FLODDEN FIELD

Elisabeth McNeill titles available from Severn House Large Print

Turn of the Tide
The Storm
Press Relations
The Lady of Cawnpore
Hot News

FLODDEN FIELD

Elisabeth McNeill

Severn House Large Print
London & New York

This first large print edition published 2009
in Great Britain and the USA by
SEVERN HOUSE PUBLISHERS LTD of
9-15 High Street, Sutton, Surrey, SM1 1DF.
First world regular print edition published 2007 by
Severn House Publishers Ltd., London and New York.

British Library Cataloguing in Publication Data

McNeill, Elisabeth
  Flodden Field : a novel. - Large print ed.
  1. James, IV, King of Scotland, 1473-1513 - Fiction
  2. Flodden, Battle of, England, 1513 - Fiction 3. Scotland
  - History - James IV, 1488-1513 - Fiction 4. Historical
  fiction 5. Large type books
  I. Title
  823.9'14[F]

  ISBN-13: 978-0-7278-7742-0

Printed and bound in Great Britain by
MPG Books Ltd, Bodmin, Cornwall.

THANKS TO:

Alex Merry, for invaluable research.

James Douglas Bell, for a wealth of information.

James Pringle, 14th Laird of Torwood-lee, descendant of Isabella Hoppringle, for information about his family.

C.G. Hallam-Baker, who brought the battlefield to life.

Kenneth Gunn, an authority on Selkirk.

Foreword

When I returned to live in the Scottish Borders after an absence of twenty-five years, I bought an old farm house called Harrietsfield thinking it had been named after some woman who lived there long ago.

In fact I discovered from a philologist that the original name was 'Heriotsfield', but it had been anglicized during the time when Scots words were frowned upon by the middle classes.

A 'heriot' was a ground rent of a fighting man, payable by the tenant of a farm whenever his feudal superior went to war, and feudal superiors in the Borders often took up arms.

My house would provide a man to fight whenever called upon to do so.

That fired my imagination, and, because the original building at Harrietsfield was very old indeed, it probably sent a man to the disastrous battle of Flodden. Was he one of the few who managed to return?

Growing up in the Borders, and being very interested in history, I was always fascinated by the battle of Flodden. Every time I drove past the range of hills where it took place, it struck me as unbelievably tragic that so many local men, including perhaps the poor soldier from Harrietsfield, died within sight of the three Eildon Hills which dominate the landscape of the eastern Borders.

An old Borderer who looked after my garden at Harrietsfield once told me that he 'didnae feel easy in his mind' when he was out of sight of the Eildons, and I knew what he meant because they exert a strange, almost magical magnetic pull over the surrounding landscape.

For years I made occasional trips to Flodden and climbed to the monument, which I have since discovered is not actually on the real site of the battle but slightly too far to the west and too low down the hill. I visited the church at Branxton as well and stood in the porch where King James' body lay among the piles of dead. The atmosphere there is so evocative and moving it was inevitable that one day I would write a novel about James IV and his disastrous venture.

Go to the Northumbrian village of Branxton and try to imagine bodies piled high after the disastrous battle that only lasted just over two hours but claimed the lives of sixty-six Scotsmen for every one English-man.

James IV perfectly embodied both the glamour and the failings of his family. The fatal flaw which made him ignore all advice and act on impulse, rushing headlong into the middle of the fighting when he should have held back, evinced itself again in his granddaughter the beautiful but rash Mary, Queen of Scots, and two hundred years later in the feckless 'Bonny' Prince Charlie, defeated at Culloden, another blood bath.

In my account of the battle, I call it Flodden though it is also often referred to as the battle of Branxton Heights. I prefer the word 'Flodden', which seems to derive from 'flood', which perfectly describes the morass into which James led his men to their destruction.

Branxton Heights is the low range of hills on which his army, and the army of his treacherous ally Lord Home, established themselves. If they had stayed in place, they would probably have prevailed.

I have stayed faithful to the Julian calendar, which is how events would be dated at the time. Scotland changed over to the Gregorian calendar, which adds eleven days, in 1582. England did not change till 1752.

I have also taken liberties by imagining some of the characters and motives of the people involved. The dramatic facts however

9

need little embroidering.

The title of the book is taken from an old Border song mourning the tragedy, 'O, Flodden Field'.

One

Tall and thin, dressed in a dark cloak and a black bonnet with a wilting plume, he strode past the darkened booths around St Giles and headed down Edinburgh's deserted High Street. In his right hand was a brass bell that he swung at regular intervals, its loud peal shattering the silence of the summer midnight and reverberating off the high stone walls of noblemen's houses in the Cannongate.

As he walked along on his skeleton legs, he called out the names of Scotland's finest families and gave a terrible warning ... 'Douglas, Fleming, Murray, Stewart and Donald – BEWARE! Go not to war or you will all die. Argyll, Hay, Graham, Rothesay and Bothwell, sheathe your swords. Marching out will kill all your best men. BEWARE!'

All the way down the steep street he shouted his terrible message, startling rats from rubbish heaps and waking huddled beggars

11

who sat up, drew their rags round their shoulders and stared at him in horror thinking they were seeing one of the many ghosts that haunted the city.

At some of the bigger houses, peepholes clicked open as he passed and watchmen's eyes blinked blearily behind the metal grilles, but he never looked their way or ceased his steady pacing. When the watchers saw that he was armed with a broadsword and looked more than capable of using it, they closed the peepholes and checked the bars behind the doors, for Edinburgh's High Street had seen many midnight killings and no one was keen to add to the number.

When he reached the courtyard of the new Palace at Holyrood that the King was building beside the ancient abbey at the foot of the Royal Mile, he swung his bell in a full circle and yelled at the pitch of his lungs, 'Are ye in there, Jamie Stewart? Hearken to me. Go not to war. If you cross the Tweed, you'll never see your native land again...'

His voice split the night like a sword thrust and a startled guard ran out and tried to grapple with him. 'Go home, madman, or you'll end up with my dagger in your belly,' he warned.

The stranger held off the guard with one hand and stared at him balefully, before saying, 'You'll die too if you follow the King into England.'

The guard seemed indifferent to this threat and said, 'Off wi' ye. I don't listen to madmen. Go home or you'll be the first to die.'

The intruder stiffened his chest and stared into the man's angry face. Then he suddenly asked in a quieter voice, 'What's your name, lad?'

Taken by surprise the guard replied, 'Robbie Mackay.'

'How old are ye?'

'Twenty.' The guard felt as if he was mesmerized by the piercing eyes that stared into his face.

'Alas, Robbie Mackay. Your time is nearly up. Your blood will flow in an English burn if you follow the King into England...'

Mackay felt a cold chill run down his back. Only that night he and his friends had been toasting the news that Jamie, their popular king, was about to lead them into a war against the English. For a panicked moment he debated stabbing this messenger of doom through the heart but there was something so weirdly intimidating about the earnest white face staring fixedly at him that he drew back his sword arm and gave him only a warning. 'Go quietly home *now* and don't disturb the King's peace or you'll be the one to die and your blood will run in an Edinburgh gutter.'

The bell-ringer sighed and shook his head as he said, 'Your soul will have my prayers,

Robbie Mackay,' before he walked away without a backward glance.

A guttering candle flickered by the bedside in the finest of the newly furbished rooms overlooking the courtyard. Plump Margaret Tudor, Queen of Scotland, sat up in alarm when she was wakened by the shouting beneath her window. It did not take her entirely by surprise because she had been warned that a message was to be delivered to the King soon. Ringing out in the darkness of a moonless midnight, however, it sounded more dreadful and convincing than she had envisaged.

Not only that, but he had come at the wrong time. Her fists curled angrily when she remembered that the man who was meant to hear the message was not in bed with her. She knew he was at Linlithgow Palace with one of his paramours. How typical of him to be absent and miss the carefully arranged warning against warmongering.

Jealous rage rose in her and she inwardly fumed, 'How dare he treat me, the daughter of one English king and sister of another, with such indifference. How dare he flaunt his preference for other women in front of the whole court!'

She was only thirteen when she first set eyes on Jamie Stewart. That was ten years ago, and she fell in love with him immediately.

Lonely in her matrimonial bed she remembered how magnificent he looked in scarlet and cloth of gold when he rode up to her litter and held out his hand to help her onto the pillion behind his saddle for their first triumphal ride into Edinburgh in the summer of 1503.

She remembered the stomach churning helpless desire that struck her then, for, like her brother Henry, she was of a highly amorous nature even at so young an age. This man who was to be her husband was so gloriously handsome that she melted at the very sight of him.

She was a spoiled eldest daughter, cosseted and flattered by all her family, and especially by her father, the fearsome Henry VII, who seized the English throne after defeating Richard III at the Battle of Bosworth Field.

When he first told her a marriage was arranged between her, his favourite daughter, perhaps even favourite child, and the King of Scotland, she demurred when she learned that he was seventeen years older than she was. Thirty seemed ancient to a girl of thirteen and she wept, saying, 'You're sacrificing me and giving me to an old man for the sake of a treaty!' She was well aware that the marriage was to seal a peace between two warring countries. The marriage of the Thistle and the Rose, they called it.

She was a pawn in a political game.

Her concerned father reassured her. 'No, no, peace is a good thing but I would not marry you off only for that. They tell the Stewart has a kind nature and will treat you well. If he does not, I'll bring you back home and punish him and his country severely.'

'But he's *old*.' Her head was full of the tales told by ladies of her household about the pleasures of love with a vigorous young man.

'He's only thirty and he looks younger than his years. They also say he's very vigorous,' her father told her and she knew she had to accept.

Escorted by the old Earl of Surrey, and with an enormous entourage of courtiers, she travelled to Scotland in 1503 still full of trepidation. The only diversion she found to stop herself dreading what lay ahead was a magnificently illustrated Book of Hours that her father presented to her before she left home.

He inscribed it with a loving message which she knew was his pledge to give her sanctuary if her marriage was a failure.

As soon as she saw James, however, her father's choice of a husband was vindicated. Though she'd grown up in a glorious court, she had never seen such a handsome, charismatic man. She stared in delight at his finely featured face, his strong beaked nose and red beard that made a striking contrast with his

16

flowing and gloriously curling black hair.

After their wedding ceremony in the beautiful Chapel Royal at Holyrood, she was even more dazzled by the tremendous display that her new husband made to celebrate the marriage. He was courtly and made her feel very special, very important and very much wanted as they sat together and watched the entertainments, pageants, jousts, concerts and acrobatic displays arranged in her honour. Conjurers and tumblers were called in to perform before her during almost every waking hour of her day.

She remembered sitting in her bridal finery, trying to look grown up for five days, while magnificent banquets were held in her honour and the large square in front of Holyrood Palace was given over to jousting and tilting, in which her new husband played a prominent part.

Because he knew she was fond of music, James had even commissioned Robert Carver, one of the most famous musicians of the day, to compose motets in her honour which were performed in the Holyrood's Chapel Royal. She felt giddy with all the attention paid to her.

The courtiers who came with her in the entourage from England were also deeply impressed when they learned that the pomp and pageantry had cost the King of Scotland over six thousand pounds, a tremendous sum, and the largest ever spent on any royal marriage in Europe.

Margaret was a typical Tudor, who not only had as strong a sexual drive as her brother but also shared her father's veneration for money. When such a fortune was lavished on her wedding, a bride could only feel both important and desirable.

Life was idyllic for the first year of her marriage because she was reckoned to be too young to have sexual intercourse and James treated her like a toy, visiting her rooms almost every day, playing cards and making music with her and above all, making her relish her growing womanliness because of his flirting. She eagerly measured her swelling breasts and watched every morning for the first signs of menstrual blood, which seemed very slow in appearing. She was fourteen when it came, and ecstatic with anticipation.

Her delight did not last long and she came down to earth a week later when he came to her bed. Shrewd and sharp-eyed, she watched his face while her maids unlaced her and stripped off her elaborate outer layers of clothing and knew instantly from the momentary flicker of disappointment he could not hide that she was not to his taste.

The court ladies knew it too and it did not take long before she started to hear stories about her husband. The more malicious women in her retinue told her that he was a man with much amatory experience and many mistresses but he did not lust after plump little girls with butter-yellow hair. His taste was for dark-haired, tall, lean women with witty tongues, women who looked like hunting dogs with long legs and skinny bodies.

His favourite mistress, she learned, Margaret Drummond, by whom he had several children (and was rumoured to have married), looked like that.

Though the Drummond woman was dead, mysteriously poisoned, James had never forgotten her, and his wife's pink, soft body and fulsome breasts were all right for a childish plaything but not for sensual pleasure. That he found elsewhere. She was not to his taste, but unfortunately, after their first night together, he was very much to hers.

Though her husband's lovemaking was only perfunctory it was frequent till she fell quickly pregnant, but from then on her marriage was a disappointment. Though her new husband was courteous, and still came frequently to her rooms to chat and make music with her, he only visited her bed to get a legitimate heir and not for mutual pleasure.

As soon as she was pregnant, James left her alone and she was forced to accept that he would never truly desire her. Frustration and jealousy made her the self-protective and querulous woman who started up when the strange bell-ringer began shouting below her window.

When the noise he made died away, she stuck her feet out of bed feeling for her slippers and slipped through the door into a narrow passage that led to the room where her infant son lay asleep in his cradle with two nursemaids and a lady of the court watching over him. All three women looked blearily up when the Queen appeared beside them and one said, 'He sleeps soundly, my lady.'

'That noise didn't wake him?' Margaret asked, leaning over the precious child, the only one of the children she had carried in her womb to survive the first few weeks of life. Her first child died very soon, as did the four who followed him, and all subsequent lovemaking with her husband was business-like and swiftly over but passionate desires and longings raged inside her and she burned with frustration when she heard of James's other love affairs.

She was fecund and fell with child six times in ten years. Miraculously this son, another James, had reached the age of sixteen months and was thriving. His mother and the whole court watched over him obsessively while his father made frequent pilgrimages to Whithorn Abbey to pray for his son's continued well-being. It was essential to him that Margaret's son was a healthy heir to the Stewart crown.

'What noise?' asked a surprised lady in waiting, who had not heard the bell-ringer because the baby's room was at the back of the palace overlooking the park.

'A man was outside beneath my window shouting a warning that the King and the Scots nobles will all be killed if they go to war against my brother,' Margaret told her. 'He called out the name of your family the Flemings when he listed those who would die.' She knew that Mary Fleming, the lady in waiting, occasionally shared Jamie's bed and was gratified when the woman's hand flew to her mouth in alarm for her father and three brothers were already preparing to join the King in his foolish venture planned against England.

'Don't worry. He sounded more like a madman than a seer, but he *was* very insistent,' Margaret said, bending over her child's cradle. Thank God, she thought, that this son was healthy and would one day be as handsome as his father, long-limbed and dark-haired. This baby, the next King of Scotland, was the justification for her existence in the court and even if Jamie was rash enough to march into England and get himself killed, she would be the mother of

21

the next ruler and still first lady in the land. If the warning bell-ringer was right, her time of power might come very soon, though she did not wish her husband dead. She still loved him and hoped that one day he would love her back.

She sounded imperious as she turned back from the cradle and told the watching women, 'Prepare my son for travelling tomorrow. We go to Linlithgow to meet his father.'

Two

Bishop William Elphinstone hated being old. His intellect was still sharp but even on this sunny July morning his bones and back ached and his hands trembled uncontrollably when he held them out to bless the people crowding admiringly round him. The three-day journey from Aberdeen to Linlithgow had been exhausting but he was compelled to come, because he had to try to stop capricious and impulsive Jamie Stewart committing the greatest folly of his life.

Grey-faced but gloriously dressed in his episcopal robes and mitre, he sat in a carved armchair by the side of a magnificent new fountain in the central courtyard of the palace the King was rebuilding in Linlithgow. Instead of water, white wine gushed liberally from the fountain's jets and some of it splashed over the paving at the bishop's feet. When the King saw him drawing back the skirts of his finely embroidered cope to prevent them being soiled, he laughed and said, 'That wine won't spoil your finery, Elphinstone. It's the best France can supply.'

The bishop pulled a disapproving face. 'You are too prodigal, my lord. Not only are you putting wine into water fountains but you're spending too much money building palaces all over Scotland.' It was true; not content with glorifying Linlithgow, James' builders were also at work on a beautiful new residence at Falkland, as well as making a range of fine chambers at Stirling Castle. The old abbey of Holyrood also had been transformed into a palace that rivalled anything to be seen in France.

James Stewart took the old man's criticism lightly, laughed and shrugged. 'My country is rich and my treasury is full,' he said.

'It will not stay that way if you go on wasting money. Spending on palaces and massive warships, allying yourself with France, gathering up an army to take on the English, hauling cannons halfway across Scotland is expensive...'

'Not to mention founding a university in your honour in Aberdeen, and setting up a medical school there as good as any in Europe,' retorted James, walking quickly away to hide the exasperation that too often rose in him these days whenever he met his old mentor and friend.

At one time Elphinstone had been more than a father to him, sharing his enthusiasms and encouraging his love of learning, but since the old man entered his eighties he'd retreated into excessive religiosity and with it came a tendency to argue with and contradict his royal protégé.

As the King walked away, his wife Margaret came across and sat beside Elphinstone. 'You look tired, your grace,' she told him in a low and sympathetic voice, almost a whisper.

His long face was deeply lined, the cheeks sagging and the nose jutting forward like that of a corpse. 'I am tired, very tired and more than a little frightened,' he admitted.

The sharp eyes set in her plump, girlish face stared questioningly at him as she sighed and asked, 'Surely not frightened? Not you.' She shivered because she remembered that Elphinstone had a reputation as a necromancer who could see into the future. They had talked about the King's warmongering before, and she knew the bishop was doing all he could to prevent her husband's projected unprovoked excursion into England.

He noted the signs of strain on her face, and knew, like him, she was frightened too. 'I'm very frightened about the calamity the King is about to bring upon himself and on Scotland if he goes to make war on your brother,' he told her.

Although as a rule he did not like women, Elphinstone recognized Margaret as an ally. He knew she was unlearned and no intellectual, but she had a good measure of her father's cold shrewdness, and Henry VII always impressed Elphinstone as being one of the most effectual rulers and tacticians who ever sat on the English throne. Like him, his daughter had a basic drive to survive and would overcome all obstacles to keep herself and her infant son safe.

By encouraging and protecting her, Elphinstone reckoned he would at least be able to ensure the continuity of the Stewart line.

She leaned close to him and whispered even lower. 'Your man came to Holyrood three nights ago and stood in the courtyard shouting warnings about the men who would die if my husband breaks the treaty of Perpetual Peace and takes up arms against my brother Henry's army.'

He fixed his sharp old eyes on her face. 'What makes you think he was my man?' he asked.

She said nothing, only stared into his eyes

till he asked another question, 'How did Jamie react?'

'He was not in my bed that night,' she said flatly.

It was his turn to sigh. 'I feared that, so I must try again,' he told her.

Behind the bishop's throne a procession was forming, and he rose stiffly to his feet to lead it into the chapel where he was to elevate the host and bless the gathering. Though the service was to ask for success in war, Elphinstone deliberately made no reference to the King's intention of leading his nobles into battle.

Because of his frailty the service was not long, and when he led the congregation back out into the sunshine, he saw a blond young man in a rough homespun blue shirt staring at him from the middle of a crowd of onlookers. The bishop dropped his eyes in a secret signal.

The King, walking behind him, looked as sleek as an otter and was gloriously dressed in purple and gold. Precious stones glittered and shone in the jewelled collar round his neck and from the many rings he wore on his fingers. One of them was an enormous sapphire, which had been sent to him as a token of love by the Queen of France, who was trying to recruit his help in France's campaign against the English. Her bribe seemed to have succeeded because he was set on going to war with it on his finger.

James was within a few strides of the door into the great dining hall when the yellow-haired young man ran up to him and cried out, 'Stay in Scotland, Jamie Stewart!'

James halted in mid-stride and stared at the importunate fellow.

'Do not advise your king,' he thundered.

'If you go into England, your son will be King,' was the reply.

This disturbed James, who suffered from a great guilt about conniving with the nobles who murdered his own father when he, the heir, was only fifteen years old.

He threateningly put a hand on the hilt of the dagger at his waist but the stranger did not back away or display any sign of retaliation, only throwing his arms wide to show he carried no weapon. A knight of chivalry could never kill an unarmed man and James was very chivalric, so his hand fell loosely by his side.

The young man fixed his eyes on Stewart's proud face and said in a loud voice, 'I warn thee, my king. Stay at peace and meddle with no women nor use their counsel, nor let them not touch thy body nor thou theirs, for if thou do it, thou will be confounded and brought to disaster...'

Onlookers were still gasping with shocked surprise at this extraordinary speech as the stranger elbowed his way through the crowd, and ran at full tilt out of the courtyard, disappearing into a throng of townspeople watching through the open gate.

Though flustered the King gathered his composure in a second and strode on into the palace dining hall, throwing himself down into a finely carved chair at the high table between the chairs pulled out for Elphinstone and the Queen. When they were also seated, he spoke to her first. 'I failed to notice if that messenger of doom spoke with an English accent, my lady. What did you think?'

Her face flushed scarlet. 'Husband, believe me, I know nothing about him.'

Smiling but still hard-eyed, James turned to the old man on his other side. 'The warning about women sounded like one of your favourite lectures, my old friend.' He wished it was possible to resurrect the admiration and respect with which he once held the old man, but since the mysterious poisoning of Margaret Drummond, the woman he loved most in the world, he could not clear his mind of a lurking suspicion that Elphinstone might have been behind her death. If she had stayed alive, he would never have entered into the Tudor alliance, which Elphinstone so dearly desired for what he wanted for Scotland was peace and an end to ancient feuding.

'Perhaps you will pay more attention to

that voice from the occult than to my words,' was the bishop's sharp reply.

It took the King a huge effort not to burst out in rage and ask, 'Did you kill my Meg twelve years ago so that the way would be clear for marriage with this unappealing woman who sits beside me now?'

Instead he allowed himself a less provocative reply. 'You talk about the occult? I do not believe in the occult any more than you do. But messengers have to be paid and told what to say. I want to know who put the words into that madman's mouth? Was it you, my old master, or my loving wife?'

Margaret's head drooped and Elphinstone said nothing. He knew that James suspected him of the mysterious poisoning of Margaret Drummond and her three sisters in 1501. At their communal burials in Dunkeld Abbey the accusation had almost slipped from the King's mouth and though he held his tongue, Elphinstone knew the breach between them opened then. It was obvious in James' stricken eyes and it still lurked there.

Because he was still alive Elphinstone knew the King was not certain of his guilt, and there were other suspects. Many people, including Henry VII, had reason to want rid of the Drummond woman. It was possible, even probable, that she and James were secretly married, and she had certainly borne him several children who he openly acknowledged. Against Elphinstone's advice, James' oldest son Alexander had been created Archbishop of St Andrews when he was only twelve years old. Now grown up, and carefully educated abroad with Erasmus one of his tutors, he was his father's favourite male companion.

For himself Elphinstone suspected Henry VII of being implicated in Margaret Drummond's death because she stood in the way of James' marriage with his daughter. Crafty old Henry was more than capable of organizing the removal of the Drummond girls. And not only him, there were also several Scottish lords who hated the Drummond family's influence on the King, and would certainly not hesitate to get rid of the woman who had the royal ear.

The old man wondered how to get James to believe that though he was greatly in favour of the alliance with England through marriage between James and Margaret, he had not ordered the killing of the King's beloved. But that was impossible and mutual respect between the two men had died with the girl.

Three

Next morning the bishop watched from his window in the palace while the King and the grandees of his court mounted their horses in the courtyard below. James was obviously in a high state of excitement and as Elphinstone stared down at him, he realized that his King was living in the past. He was still in the days of knights in armour and chivalric wars but the world was changing.

'I am an old man, but I know it. He is young and he is oblivious,' he said to his grim-faced secretary, Drysdale, who stood by his side in the window embrasure.

'Know what?' asked Drysdale.

'About the world changing around us,' was the bishop's reply.

'James is too headstrong to listen to any advice,' said Drysdale.

'And he's going to Edinburgh after all,' said the bishop in a dispirited voice.

'Once he gets an idea in his mind nothing will shift it, but at least he hasn't made a declaration of war yet,' was the reply.

'He will, he will. His father was impulsive

too. He listened to no advice and they killed him for it. I'm afraid this one is doomed as well, if not this year, then in the near future. He's a typical Stewart and no Stewart king has ever died in his bed,' Elphinstone told him.

'But he has so many talents,' said the secretary, who admired the handsome, volatile King.

'If anything he has too many. Clever, charming, quick-witted, artistic and courteous. A very perfect knight – but flawed by impetuosity, and that bastard son of his, St Andrews, is just like him,' Elphinstone sighed, pointing at an upright young man standing by the King's horse.

'Yes, he is his father's son as far as talents are concerned, and just as lascivious,' agreed the secretary. He disliked the swaggering young illegitimate son, who was always surrounded by a pack of fawning hangers-on.

'His father would like him to be next on the throne but that's not to be unless murder is done again. He's done his best for the bastard boy, though. He persuaded the Borgia Pope to make him an archbishop because he couldn't be a king. I wonder, what will the Tudor woman's child be like? Sometimes I wish I was immortal to know what will happen after I am dead.' Death was much on Elphinstone's mind those days.

'As long the new prince doesn't turn out like her posturing brother,' said Drysdale.

Elphinstone smiled wryly. 'Let us pray he takes after her cunning father, then,' he said and turned away from the window as the noise of horses' hooves on stone told him the cavalcade was leaving. 'I must take my leave of her now before we go.'

Drysdale pursed his lips and said, 'She's a trivial-minded woman. If she did not complain so much about her brother keeping part of her dowry, the King would have no excuse for this mad enterprise.'

'It's not all her fault. This new enterprise is not only about her jewellery. Jamie is making use of her dowry grievances for his own ends. He has other reasons for war. He wants to recapture Berwick and he sees himself as another Bruce, defeating the English, driving them out of the north. He's out for his own glory and the French are wooing him to attack England because they want to sting Henry Tudor in the tail now that he's posturing about in their country. Some Scottish lords are as keen on going to war as James is. He's fretting for glory and so are they. They see this as their chance to hit the English and aggrandize themselves. Margaret's dowry is only a convenient excuse. I've told him to forget it.'

Elphinstone knew that the magnates who had James' ear also told him not to listen to the old bishop, hinting he was an agent for the English and protector of the killers of Margaret Drummond.

'Let us hope that my worst fears are not justified,' he ended sadly before he went to take his leave of the Queen and her baby son. It was to be their last meeting.

Four

At the end of July, the city of Edinburgh was stricken by a visitation of the plague and most of the people living in the high tenements that lined the road between the palace of Holyrood and the castle perched on its rocky outcrop stayed in their homes with doors barred to keep out strangers who might carry in the infection.

When it broke out anyway in one of the narrow alleys running off the High Street, it was walled off at both ends and the inhabitants left to die of the disease or starve to death. Even that draconian measure failed to halt the progress of the scourge.

Only the brave or the indifferent ventured out of doors and they were the first to hear news of the vast gathering of armed men who were advancing towards them under the

King's banner. Terrified of the effect this host would have on their peace and prosperity, the burgesses and rich merchants sent a messenger to the King to advise him not to enter Edinburgh because it was ravaged by plague. James turned aside and ordered his army to encamp on Boroughmuir, a vast expanse of open ground on the south side of the city.

From the attics of twenty-storey tenements and the turrets of the castle, men stared out and spied what looked like a black mass of ants crowding into the green space beyond the city boundaries. The numbers of the crowd increased every day and word spread that the King had given orders to summon men from all over Scotland to follow him into battle against the ancient enemy, England. His feudal summons extended to Edinburgh as well and the burgesses were told to provide a big fighting force.

It was rumoured that a hundred thousand men were mustered at Boroughmuir ready to follow the King into England. 'A hundred thousand!' people gasped to each other, for the whole city of Edinburgh had a population of only seventeen thousand and always seemed crowded.

As the mass at Boroughmuir grew daily bigger the curious citizenry could contain themselves no longer and came out in their hundreds to see what was going on. They were very self-protective people, not partisan for any king or even any country, but what they saw made even the most cautious heart rise with patriotic fervour because the scene spread before them could have been copied from a mediaeval tapestry.

Over an area of more than two square miles were line upon line of white tents with pointed roofs from the central poles of which flew baronial flags in a myriad of colours. Armed men and horses milled about everywhere. Men sang and music played. It was more like a celebration than a war gathering.

Though the army might not really be the rumoured one hundred thousand strong, it was at least twenty-five thousand and that was sufficiently enormous to impress the spectators, who stayed off the field and gawped at armed men, ranging from Swiss pikemen in shining armour to tangle-haired, bare-legged Highlanders in rough plaids carrying claymores or Lochaber axes clustering round their clan chiefs. These heathen-looking men stared with hostility at Lowlanders, who could not understand a word they said.

There were rich burgesses from Glasgow who kept themselves apart from their equivalent grandees of Edinburgh, for the two cities were always at loggerheads. Men in search of adventure and rogues in search of someone to rob mingled with the throng, all waiting for the summons of their king, who was boldly quartered in the castle that loomed on the horizon above their heads.

At midday on July 24th, he rode across the castle drawbridge on a huge dappled war horse and thrust his spurs into its sides to make it gallop down the steep hill to the south. When he saw the huge crowd spread out before him at Boroughmuir, he yelled, 'make way for the King,' and galloped onto the field so that men had to scatter like flies before him.

As he passed a crowd of Camerons grouped protectively around their lord of Lochiel, he raised one arm and greeted them in Gaelic. Delighted, they greeted him back, blessing him and assuring him of their loyalty. No other Scottish king in living memory had taken the trouble to learn Gaelic and they loved him for it, not knowing that he was equally fluent in French, German, Spanish, Italian and Portuguese.

A group of knights cleared a way for him to climb onto the flat bed of a two-wheeled cart and he stood up there with both arms outspread and his long black hair flowing from beneath a scarlet bonnet while his standard-bearer unfurled his personal banner, a flag of cloth of gold emblazoned with a black wing-spreading falcon, and raised it above his head. While the crowd cheered, he shouted at the pitch of his lungs, 'Victory will be ours. We will drive the English out of Berwick, out of Northumberland. March south to Coldstream and wait there for me...

'I'm going to gather in my men of the Borders and sack the first English stronghold, Norham Castle. When I cross the Tweed into England, follow me.'

He paused to stare around and then went on. 'My master of gunnery Robert Borthwick is bringing cannons to the Border that will blast the Englishmen out of every northern stronghold they possess. Victory will be ours. You will all be heroes.'

The effect he had on the crowd was instant and enormous. Without thinking of the dangers or consequences they began whooping and yelling in ecstasy. James's heart was racing and he was transfixed with pride and excitement as he stared out at the sea of faces before him, young faces and old faces, smiling faces and serious ones too. He felt like a boy again.

The scent of battle was in his nostrils and he almost burst into tears when he saw the vast gathering of men who had turned out in response to his summons.

He turned his face up to the sky and raised his arms above his head. 'God is with us!' he cried and a wave of cheers came from the crowd round his feet and spread back into the masses crowding behind them.

He had no doubts about this great enterprise. At his disposal would be the largest army ever assembled in Scotland. It could outnumber anything England could raise by at least four to one because Henry Tudor's main army was away fighting in France, and only a garrison remained at home under the control of the Earl of Surrey, a man in his seventies. It was doubtful if Surrey could summon up ten thousand men altogether and the Scots had more than that number here already with many more to come as they headed south.

The Earl of Home had promised to raise at least another ten thousand men from the Borders, and contingents of French pikemen and Swiss foot soldiers, sent over from France, were already waiting near Coldstream. The highly disciplined Swiss were armed with eight-foot-long halberds and were reckoned to be the finest fighting men in Europe.

There was no doubt in his mind that he would win glory for Scotland. The name of James Stewart would be forever remembered. He would become a legend like the Bruce and his country would be among the most powerful in the world.

Standing at the edge of the crowd, the Provost of Edinburgh glanced at the companion by his side and said in a low voice, 'He's hysterical. Is this enterprise properly thought out, do you suppose? For one thing, how does he plan to feed this horde when it's on the march?'

'He has a huge baggage train. Merchants have been gathering up food all week and rubbing their hands at the profit they're making. The men who are called on to follow the army have been told to carry forty days' food on their backs – oatmeal and salt herring as far as the Highlanders are concerned, but a lot of them will depend on pillage. They'll help themselves as they go along. If you and I have to go we'd better organize our own supplies and made sure they're fresh,' was the answer.

'And well guarded. I can assure you that I won't be around long enough to worry about pillaging. As soon as we reach Coldstream, I'll be on my way home on the fastest horse I can find. You should do the same. We'll have answered the royal summons, and fulfilled our obligations. I'm sure he won't miss us. We'd be better back in Edinburgh defending our own city, anyway. Who's to say the English won't attack us while James is battling on the Border?' said the Provost.

The other man nodded vigorously in total agreement.

Five

Magdalen Fletcher was kneading bread dough in her kitchen when a king's messenger came clattering and shouting into the square of the Border royal burgh of Selkirk. She stepped out of her door and bumped into her sister-in-law Ellen, who lived next door.

'What's all the noise about? What's happening?' she asked.

'He's yelling something about a call to arms,' said Ellen.

Magdalen, who was younger and more timid than Ellen, dusted flour off her bare arms, and looked scared. 'Arms? Fighting? How will that affect us?' she asked.

'It's a king's summons. My father told me about one that came when he was a lad. Our burgesses will have to send men to fight for the King.'

'How many men? Where will they have to go?'

Ellen shrugged. 'I dinna ken. It depends. If the King's going to war, they'll have to go with him.'

'How many of them?'

Magdalen was on the verge of tears and Ellen tried to reassure her. 'About ten, I suppose, but even the King can't keep them away for more than forty days. I mind my father saying that's the rule.'

'Forty days!' That seemed like an eternity to newly married Magdalen. All sorts of terrible things could happen to her beloved husband Edward in forty days if he was taken away to fight battles for the King. Edward, a shoemaker in the town, wasn't the fighting type.

The women walked down a little alleyway from their front doors to the open space in front of the church, where men were gathering round a man on a sweating horse. Someone passed him up a mug of ale and others were beleaguering him with questions. When he'd taken a large draught from the mug, he jumped out of the saddle and said, 'It's the royal summons. The King is marching into England and Selkirk has to raise eighty men between the ages of sixteen and sixty to go with him.'

Consternation broke out. 'Eighty men,' shouted several voices in protest, 'there's only a hundred able men in the toon!' Others arrived in the square, some running, and they too cried out in dismay when the news was broken to them.

The messenger regarded them impassively.

He was used to a bad reception. 'How you get the men is up to you,' he told them, 'all I know is that Selkirk has to send eighty men and there's no getting out of it. Meet up with Home's men when he sends you his summons. It won't be long.'

Then he laid his mug on the ground, and remounted to go to the next stop with his unwelcome news.

When he clattered away, the men in the square, all in their working clothes and varying states of cleanliness, started arguing among themselves while the women stood aside watching, some of them twisting their aprons in their hands with anxiety. It was a long time since there was any serious fighting near Selkirk and they had little stomach for it.

The Fletcher family was one of the most prominent in the town and Robert, the eldest of six brothers, was the provost, in charge of keeping peace and administering the law. All eyes turned to him.

'He says it's war with England and we've to go there,' said Williamson, the big blacksmith.

Robert nodded. 'Aye, we've to join up with Home's men outside Duns and then march on to Coldstream.'

Coldstream was on the border between England and Scotland. Few of the Selkirk men had ever been there.

'And he wants eighty men from us,' said Williamson again.

'It'll be good work for you, Rob,' said sly-eyed Gillie, the town butcher.

'What do ye mean?' asked Robert angrily.

'If the King's going to war think aboot a' the arrows that'll be shot off here, there and everywhere,' said Gillie and someone at the back of the crowd laughed because Robert Fletcher made his living by skilfully putting the feathers on arrows, as his name indicated.

Robert waved a hand to signify that Gillie was wasting time. 'Are you up for going?' he asked the butcher.

'I canna go. I'm ower auld. I'm sixty-one,' was the reply. Gillie was safe.

'Where are we going to get eighty fighting men?' queried Robert's brother Edward.

'We have to. It's our feudal due. We're a royal burgh and we've got to provide eighty armed and mounted men between the ages of sixteen and sixty for forty days. So start counting. Who's going?' said Richard Fletcher, Ellen's husband, who worked as a baker.

Nobody was enthusiastic and all started giving reasons why they couldn't leave home – sick wives, imminent births, heavy work-loads, ageing parents were all offered as excuses but Robert shouted them down. 'There's no getting out of it. We have to send eighty men.'

'Not all from Selkirk, surely? We're only a wee town. If eighty of us go there won't be a fit man left in the place. Who else will make up our numbers?' asked the town's lawyer.

Richard silently looked around the gathering. More than half were either old or infirm. 'We'll call up a company of archers from Ettrick Forest. That should account for fifteen or twenty and we can get another ten from Scott's lands round Bowhill. The rest of you will have to make up the levy by either going yourselves or sending your sons. We'll raise our obligation in time.'

The only faces that showed any enthusiasm for this suggestion were those of young men who were always up for an adventure and did not think themselves mortal.

'When do we go?' asked Dan, the only unmarried Fletcher, a red-headed young man who dreamed of getting out of Selkirk.

'We'll go when we get the next summons. The messenger told me he is on his way to Melrose and Dryburgh now and then he goes up the Leader valley to Earlston. Like us, they're to ride east and gather at Home's stronghold near Duns. It'll be a huge army.'

'Will they a' be from round here?' asked Dan.

'No, they'll be gathered in from a' airts. The messenger said that even a lot of Highlanders have come down from the north to fight alongside their King. They like him.'

'And they like fighting,' said Gillie acidly.

'And you don't?' asked Dan.

'No, I don't, but I'm a burgess like your brother and because I'm old my son'll go in my place. Put the word round to the others.'

By nightfall the crowd in the alehouse had grown so large that men were standing outside the door shouting comments inside.

'I've a laddie who'll go for me.'

'I'm going.'

'Aye, you'll go because there'll be booty to gather up.'

'I'll go too. It probably won't come to a fight anyway,' said an optimist.

By nine o'clock, eighty Selkirk men had either been dragooned into going or had pledged to ride out and join the King's army. As the Fletcher brothers called out their names there was one abstention. Edward sat blank-faced and silent. His brothers all stared at him. 'Say your name,' ordered Robert.

'No.'

'*No?* What do you mean, 'no'?'

'I've no stomach for war. I'm staying here,' said Edward.

Robert's face flushed scarlet. 'You're a Fletcher, one of the oldest families in the town. Don't shame us. Are you feared to fight?'

'No, I'm not feared. I'm sensible. If four of

my brothers are going that's enough for one family. Who'll take care of our widows and orphans if you're all killed?' said Edward calmly.

Robert spat on the floor. 'Coward! You're a coward!' he shouted. 'You're staying at home because you're craven and because you canna stay out of your wife's bed.' Magdalen and Edward had only been married for a year and had no children yet. All the other brothers except Dan were fathers several times over.

Scorn did not change Edward's mind, however. 'I'm staying because I've no stomach for fighting the English,' he repeated stoically.

When the church bell in the old church sounded for evening curfew, so much ale had been consumed that the whole town was bellicose and even those who had originally been reluctant to fight were won round – still with the exception of Edward, who went home sober and told Magdalen, 'My brothers are all off to fight the English soon.'

She stared at him with fear clear on her face. 'And you?'

He shook his head. 'I said no. You'll probably get a rough tongueing from some of the women for this but you're not to worry about it. I'm staying here with you.'

Word was sent up the Ettrick Valley to

recruit a contingent of archers and they arrived on the same day as the second official summons to march to Coldstream. The men of Selkirk came trooping out of their houses and made their way to the market cross in the middle of the square while women and excited children followed them proudly. Various townspeople loaned their best horses, and old broadswords had been hauled out of hiding places in rafters and sharpened and buffed up till they shone.

The burgesses of the town, including the Fletchers, were provided with round shields and steel helmets from the burgh's armoury behind the courthouse. Women had been baking bread round the clock for days and a trio of heavily laden carts carried enough provisions behind the contingent to feed the men for forty days.

The man in charge of the feed carts was the town guard, Old Tom, who had kept order and terrified all the boys of the town for forty years.

They made a brave sight, all dressed in jerkins of green, and when they were mounted, mugs of ale were passed up them and someone raised a cheer ... 'One, two, three – for our men, Selkirk and the King!'

Robert Fletcher proudly carried the town standard fluttering above his head as he and four of his brothers rode out stirrup to stirrup, first in the group. None of them cast a glance in the direction of the shoemaker's house where Edward and Magdalen could be seen standing in the open doorway.

When the last of the men disappeared through the narrow south port of the town, Ellen Fletcher turned and yelled at her brother and sister-in-law, 'Ye needna think you're going to share the booty our men bring home. We dinna share wi' cowards. You're a disgrace to the Fletcher name!'

Edward put an arm round his white-faced wife's waist and pulled her inside, slamming the door behind them while a raucous chorus of woman catcalled at their window.

'They might be glad of me one day,' he said to his wife as they closed their shutters.

Six

When he left Selkirk, the King's first messenger rode on to the great red sandstone eleventh-century abbey at Melrose, where he told the abbot that his sovereign James requested that he send a contingent of men to join his army at Duns.

The abbot raised a sceptical eyebrow. 'So he's venturing into England, is he? He'll be the aggressor if he does that.'

'He's mounting a challenge to Henry Tudor. Our army is already forty thousand strong, the largest army Scotland has ever sent to war.'

'Hmmm, with such a host James'll be able to swamp what's left of the English army, for he's chosen his time well. Henry's off fighting in France now, isn't he?'

'His army is engaged there,' agreed the messenger.

'But remember there's still a lot of men in England and Henry has left Queen Catherine and the Earl of Surrey in command. She's a fierce Spaniard and he's a shrewd man and a hardened warrior. They won't take kindly to an invasion from Scotland,' warned the abbot.

'King James has the support of all the Scottish lords,' said the messenger.

'And all the local thieves and rogues as well, though it's sometimes difficult to tell them apart. I don't relish the idea of fighting myself but, because I must, I'll find men to join the King. Make sure you call on my brother abbot at Dryburgh too. There's no reason why he should escape his feudal duties. I hope James knows what he's doing and doesn't bring English revenge down on us,' was the bleak reply.

Leaving behind the cold disapproval of the Melrose abbot, who was obviously more interested in raising sheep and supervising his many farms than fighting, the messenger rode on to Dryburgh three miles along the River Tweed, where he found a very different welcome.

As he rode under the stone entrance arch, he looked around in appreciation and thought it a pity that he was bringing news of death and battle to such a peaceful place, where the loudest noise was the cooing of doves.

Less imposing and rich than Melrose, the weathered sandstone buildings of Dryburgh seemed to be sleeping in a bower of clustering trees on the northern bank of the Tweed. Between the river and the church and clustering abbey buildings, the river's broad pastures were dotted here and there with flocks of grazing sheep that brought the monks a good income from their fine fleeces. In the abbey's walled gardens they also raised a large variety of plants and flowers, which they used for dispensing medicines. Their cures were eagerly sought after by the people living round about, especially those suffering from heart trouble because the monks made a special medicine from the snowdrops that carpeted their spring pastures in a spread of white. It was now high summer, and the snowdrops were past but the gardens were a riot of other scents and colours, particularly the red of opium poppies that made a tincture for the removal of pain.

At the narrow gate facing the river and its hidden ford, the messenger got down from his horse and led it by its bridle to an out-building, where he asked a robed brother to direct him to the abbot.

This dignitary turned out to be less con-descending and more hospitable than his equivalent in Melrose, because not only did he press food on the messenger, but gave him a night's lodging as well. He made no comment, good or bad, when he heard about the King's summons, only nodded his head slowly and said, 'I will raise the men. Where do they go and when?'

'You'll get another summons, but as soon as possible, to Ellem Kirk, the Home strong-hold at Duns. All the men from this part of the Border are to muster there.'

'And then they'll cross the Tweed at Cold-stream ford, no doubt.'

'It's the best ford on the Tweed,' agreed the messenger.

'And it's near Berwick, which the King covets,' said the abbot, who had his own theories about the King's reasons for going to war.

While the messenger slept that night, the abbot prepared to send his summons of service out to the abbey's possessions, to vil-lages, hamlets, farms and watermills spread in a ten-mile circle around about. The duty to provide a fighting man for a certain amount of acres held in tenancy was known as 'heriot' and he had a long list of them on a parchment kept on a stone shelf in his chamber. It had been a long time since it was unfolded and men sent out to fight.

The runners who took out the news of this levy were locally born lay brothers who were related to many of the people they called on.

Seventeen-year-old Robbie Smail ran two miles to Sorley's Mill at the junction of the rivers Leader and Tweed. It was owned by his uncle Alexander Purvis.

Delighted to be on the loose and away from abbey duties, he ran into the mill yard, sniffing the delicious smell of ground oats and barley, and shouting to make himself heard above the noise of the ancient wooden machinery that creaked and groaned and made the whole building shudder gently when the water-powered mill wheel turned round.

'Hey, hey, the King's going to war against the English and the abbot says you've got to send two men to fight!' he yelled.

His uncle's head popped down out of the trapdoor in the floor above the main room downstairs and he shouted back, 'Don't be silly. It's harvest time. Can't he send somebody else?'

'No, all the farms round about have to

send men as their heriot. You're lucky you've only got to provide two. Redpath farm has to send three and the folk from Sorley's farm are down for two as well!'

'Well, their heriot's fixed according to their acreage. Redpath is a big farm and there are five men there. I've only one son.'

'You've two.'

'But you canna count Thomas.'

'The abbot's counted him. He doesnae know that Thomas is wanting.'

A kitchen door opened in the mill house at Robbie's back and an indignant woman in a long white apron shouted back, 'What are you saying, Robbie? My laddie's not wanting. He's only slow.'

'Too slow to go fighting anyway,' agreed her husband the miller from above their heads.

Behind the woman in the doorway, two young girls appeared with their heads popping up above their mother's shoulders. From the grinding floor came another voice, 'But I want to go fighting. I'll tak' the old sword and kill ten Englishmen!'

'Aye, so ye will, Thomas,' said one of the girls soothingly as she stepped into the middle of the floor and stared up the wooden ladder at the open trapdoor.

The father of the family climbed down first, followed by a broadly smiling Thomas, whose flat, slant-eyed face gave a clue to his mental insufficiency. Last came the other son of the house, twenty-year-old Peter, whose hair was the colour of amber. That hair was much envied by his sisters who often moaned, 'Why did *you* get the bonny hair and we're both plain brown like sparrows!'

Peter and his father stared at the bringer of bad news and then at each other. 'Like I said, it's harvest time and who's going to run the mill?' asked the older man.

'That's why the abbot's only asked you for two men. He knows somebody must run the mill and he thought it'd be you or Peter so Thomas had to be counted as a fighting man to fulfil your heriot. Can't the old man help you out here?'

'The old man's awful feeble. He's seventy-one and half blind. It takes Peter and me and Thomas to run the mill at harvest time.'

'We'll do your work,' chorused the girls.

'It's too much for you,' said their father shortly.

'Then let me dress up as a boy and go to fight in Peter's place,' said the youngest sister, Lucy. In spite of their anxiety, everyone laughed at that.

'You needn't bother, because I'm going anyway,' said Peter firmly.

Nobody disagreed with him, but their mother wrinkled her brow and said, 'Maybe one of the wee boys from Leaderfoot farm could go for us and let us keep Thomas here. He'll be able to help his father.'

'The farm has to provide its own men,' Robbie told them.

'Besides they're all just bairns, too young for the levy. The oldest is only twelve or thirteen. If we leave Thomas at home I'll have to go and hope the fighting doesnae last long,' said the father dolefully.

Mother Purvis wrung her hands. 'Most folk have finished cutting their corn. They'll be bringing it in for grinding soon if the weather holds. You cannae be spared.'

Her husband turned on her. 'Then it'll hae to be Thomas.'

She groaned, 'Oh no, not my bairn! He's no' able to look after himself.'

Peter reached out and hugged her. 'Don't worry, Mother, I'll look after him. I'll no' let anything bad happen to him.'

'Oh, Peter, he's so trusting. He'll no' be able to tell an Englishman from a Scotsman.'

'Neither can I and I'm going too,' said young Robbie, who saw this war as an opportunity to get out of the religious life.

A solemn group of Purvises sat down to supper that night. Leaning his elbows on the table, the father of the family surveyed them all and gave his orders. 'Peter, you'll take the big bay horse and we'll bring the old grey in off the field for Thomas.'

The confused grandfather, who was sitting in a chair by the inglenook, asked querulously, 'Where's Thomas going on the grey? It's bad in the legs, like me.'

'He's only going to Duns,' said Thomas's mother soothingly. She hoped that what she said was true.

'Even that's too far for the grey.'

'Then I'll steal a horse from an Englishman,' said Thomas gleefully. Apart from Robbie, he was the only member of the family who was relishing the prospect of war.

'When are they leaving?' Lucy asked.

'Soon. When the message comes.'

'Will everybody round about go at the same time?' she asked.

'Probably. It will be best for us all to ride out together like a proper army,' said Peter.

She stood up and pulled her shawl off the back of her chair and said, 'In that case, I'm going for a walk.'

'And so am I,' said her sister Ishbel, getting up as well.

In their mother's herb garden at the back of the mill, the sisters stood and stared at each other for a few moments till Lucy asked, 'Are you going to the Lees?'

'Yes, but dinna tell Father.'

Lucy nodded in agreement. 'All right. I'm going up to Sorley's. I want to hear what the Hoggs have to say about this'

'All right. Goodbye, then.' They turned

and ran off in different directions. Above their heads the sky was streaked with scarlet, forecasting a fine day for the morrow.

Dusk was already gathering when Ishbel ran into the yard of the Lees' farm at Redpath village, a mile from the mill. There was a flickering light shining through the shutter over a tiny downstairs window and she could hear voices. Rapping on the shutter, she called, 'Sam,' and the voices inside stilled.

'Sam,' she called again and the door creaked open. Her heart leaped in her chest when she saw him standing against the light coming from the room behind. He was tall and straight with jet-black hair tumbling uncombed to his shoulders. He was dangerous-looking. Her father would be angry if he knew where she was, because he'd disliked the Lees ever since they moved into the district two years ago. He said they were gypsies, and suspected them of being horse-thieves. It had to be admitted that all four Lees brothers did have a Romany look.

'It's me, Sam,' she whispered and he came out, shutting the door behind him with one hand while he took her arm with the other and pulled her towards the hay shed.

In seconds they were lying among the hay and she was powerless as he began pulling up her skirts. When they finished their love-making, he lay back on one arm, grinning as he said, 'That was the proper way to say goodbye to me, lass.'

'So you're going to fight for the King as well?' she asked.

He nodded. 'Yes, me and my brothers. The old man stays here.'

'All four of you? Do you have to send so many?'

He laughed. 'Our heriot's for three but if there's good pickings to be had a Lee won't stay at home. There'll be plenty of plunder on a battlefield. I'll stay away long enough to come back with a golden ring for you.'

She shuddered. 'A dead man's ring?'

He laughed again. 'Don't worry. I'll pick you a good one.'

She sat up, brushing hay from her clothes, and said, 'I came to find out if you were going and to wish you good luck but there's something else I want you to know before you go. I'm almost sure I'm having your child...'

He groaned. 'Aw no. I don't want more. I've six already.'

'But you told me it was only three. You said your wife died having the last one and her mother's raising it.'

'You might as well know. Not exactly. I've six and my wife isn't dead. She went back to her mother in Lauder before I met you and she took the wee ones with her.'

She put her head in her hands. So her

father was right. She'd been a fool but Sam was the most handsome man she'd ever seen. The first time she saw him, carrying sacks of wheat into her father's mill last harvest time, she was so affected that she felt her head swim and thought she was going to faint. He spotted the effect he had on her and seduced her within a week.

'What about me and my baby?' she asked weakly.

'When I come back from the fighting, you can move in here with me. I'll say we're married. Nobody will be any the wiser. Anyway I didn't stand up in church with the other one either.'

She rose unsteadily, feeling sick, dreading what her devoutly religious father would say when he heard. Sam was still making excuses. 'You were as keen as me. I didnae have to persuade you.'

'My father'll kill you,' she whispered.

He laughed. 'The English might do that first. I'll have a word with your father when I get back. Maybe I could give him something...'

Bile rose in her throat. 'My father's not that kind of man,' she said.

Sam looked at her with cold black eyes. 'He's not in a position to bargain, is he? Tell him I'll give him a good horse if he looks after your bastard.'

Filled with shame, she was about to attack

him with her fists when an idea struck her. 'I'll tell him myself and I'll take the horse now,' she said coldly. It was as if someone had thrown a bucket of cold water over her and brought her to her senses about Sam Lee. At least she might be able to do something to temper her father's rage and disappointment. A steady horse would be a good mount for Thomas, because their old grey was lame.

Sam laughed as if she was only confirming his cynical convictions. 'Which one do you want?' he asked.

'The best one.'

'Of course.' He laughed again. 'We need four to go to Ellem Kirk but we have six in the stable right now. You can have your pick of the other two.' A slight feeling of remorse about what he'd done to her stirred inside him, and he added, 'I'll give you a chestnut mare we got last week. She's sweet-natured and a good ride for a woman. Come and see her.'

'It's not for me. It's for my brother to go to war on. Our grey's lame and my family might as well get some recompense for me having no sense and taking up with you.'

Sam was unabashed. 'The chestnut's a bit lightweight. Which brother is it for?'

'Thomas.'

'The daftie!' He laughed. 'Is the daftie going to war? He won't be joining in a cavalry charge, so the chestnut will do well enough for him. Come on, I'll get her out and you can ride her home.'

The mare was pretty and gentle and Ishbel mounted her bareback, taking the reins from Sam as he said, 'Look after her. I'll roll you in the hayshed again when I get back from the war.'

'I promise you that's one thing that won't happen,' she retorted angrily.

Seven

At the same time as her sister was riding away from the Lees' farm with tears pouring down her cheeks, in Sorley's farm a mile and a half north of the mill, Lucy burst into the kitchen and announced to the assembled Hogg family, 'Isn't it exciting! My brothers are going to fight for the King.'

Sitting round a long wooden table, they all looked up and grinned at her. 'We're going too,' said a young lad with an untidy thatch of fair hair and a kind face.

She squeezed onto a bench beside him and her eyes went from face to face. 'All of you? My grandfather's not going because of the pains in his legs and my father has to stay at

Fortunately Lucy's mother was a trusting, unsuspecting woman. 'Yes, fill a sack with our best flour. As long as you're only visiting Mary in the town you'll be safe enough. The old grey can't go far so take the back ways, away from the main track, and don't try to get to Ellem Kirk. Keep away from the army. Men in a crowd can be dangerous,' she said, wiping her hands on her apron and wondering if she should interrupt her busy husband to ask about this sudden impulse of Lucy's.

'I can look after myself,' said the girl boldly and ran out to saddle the horse before her mother had time to really contemplate the situation and perhaps stop it.

Eight

The deep purple shadows of an August evening slanted across the stone paving beneath the walkway in the cloisters of Coldstream Abbey. White doves perched on the red-tile roofs burbled contentedly as they prepared to roost for the night. Smoke spiralling up into a pink sky from the tall triple chimneys of the huge kitchen sent the smell of burning applewood and roasting meat over the town that clustered round the abbey's outer wall.

Isabella Hoppringle, the tall and imposing abbess, came sweeping down the wide stone stairs from her first-floor apartment and paused at the open doorway to stare out into the enclosed herb garden that filled the square in front of the cloisters with scent. Appreciatively she sniffed mint and rosemary, thyme and camomile but her pleasure was only fleeting, for as she appreciated the beauty of her surroundings, she was also filled with a feeling of terrible despair.

Today the abbey was so beautiful and peaceful, a place where it was possible to worship God and pray for the souls of one's fellow men, but there was another side that she could not ignore. Danger and death were approaching her threshold. The peace of this summer night was about to be smashed into pieces.

She'd known that trouble was looming for weeks because she had good contacts in Edinburgh and Linlithgow who fed her news of the doings at James' court. She had equally good contacts in England, especially those in the strongholds of the Percys and the Dacres, who had been sending news to her as well and none of it was good. They told her when Henry Tudor took his army into France to make war, and as soon as she heard that, she feared that James Stewart would be unable to resist making trouble on the Border in the English army's absence.

She was right. That very day a messenger rode in to tell her the vast Scottish army had gathered and was on the move, growing bigger with every mile it covered from Edinburgh. 'Has the King declared war on England?' she asked grimly.

'Not yet, but he means to fight and he'll be sending the declaration soon. Trouble is on its way, my lady,' was the reply.

Pondering this bad news, the stern-faced abbess walked down the central path from the cloisters to the main gate that stood welcomingly open. From it she stared down the grassy slope to the gently purling waters of the River Tweed. The water was low today, which meant the ford directly in front of the abbey would be easy to cross. That ford was James Stewart's army's highway into England. She shuddered as she looked at the silvery rippling water.

Though she was Scottish born and bred, a member of an old and influential family that maintained strongholds along the northern banks of the Tweed and into the heart of the Borderland, she was a cool-headed pragmatist and not irrationally patriotic. When it came to choosing between her country and her responsibilities as an abbess she had no problem in opting for the abbey's interests every time.

Her skill as a diplomatist and a discreet provider of information meant she stood in good favour with powerful people on both sides of the Border. Henry VIII's Spanish queen Catherine was in awe of Coldstream's abbess and openly pledged protection for her, telling the powerful lords of the north to do no damage to her or Coldstream Abbey's property.

James Stewart's Tudor wife Margaret was also a generous ally though her power to influence events was less than Catherine's.

Isabella adroitly played one interest against the other without alienating any of them because she was an invaluable source of news and information to both from her abbey perched above the ford, the salient crossing point of the Borders between the two countries. Even when no war was declared, the two nations warily eyed and feared each other from her salient position.

Her loyalties were simple – to Coldstream Abbey and Coldstream Abbey alone. She had succeeded to her position as abbess from her formidable aunt and was determined to keep its lands, its pastures, its farms, its mills and its river fishing safe and lucrative. Though she was a woman, she was a power above powerful men, Scottish and English alike.

When the soft-tongued bell rang out for the evening service, she turned and walked quickly back to the abbey church, where the twenty sisters of her order were assembled and waiting for her. She knelt and listened with only part of her mind to the priest who celebrated Mass, but mainly she was thinking about what lay ahead. Where would James attack first? English-held Norham castle was an obvious choice. If what she heard about the strength of the cannon being hauled down from Edinburgh was true, Norham would capitulate quickly.

Where would he go after that? Damn him if he brought devastation to this beautiful land. He'd either cross Twizel Bridge into England or go by Coldstream ford over the Tweed. She hoped he'd opt for Twizel and leave her alone but that was unlikely because more men could cross the ford than could squeeze over the narrow bridge. Fifty thousand men would take days to cross it.

She guessed Home would back James up because the Homes were always eager for a profitable expedition, and so were the rough Borderers who rallied under their banner. She decided to send out messengers to tell her tenants to stay at home and guard their lands. She bent her head and prayed for a quick conclusion to James' foray, however it ended.

No matter who won, Coldstream Abbey and its lands must be safe. She'd see to that. She lay down in supplication on the abbey church floor and spread her arms wide as if she was being crucified.

Among the praying nuns who surrounded her, there were some who watched their abbess more than they watched the officiating priest.

Many of them wondered about what was going on in her head, because although they were technically in a convent, they were very much in touch with events outside and most of them had powerful brothers and fathers in the lay world. They knew the abbess was in the same position.

Until she was forty, she had been married for over twenty-one years to a powerful man, Sir David Home, the Baron of Wedderburn, by whom she had seven sons, all tall and handsome like their parents, so tall and straight in fact that they were collectively known as the Spears of Wedderburn.

The marriage was not happy. Home was lecherous and uninterested in learning; Isabella was jealous and a scholar. She was also devout, which he was not. While she was still fecund, she stayed with him in the hope of producing the daughter for which she yearned, but every pregnancy gave her yet another son, each one, except the first, a copy in mind and looks of the one before.

On her fortieth birthday she told her husband that she was retiring to a convent. But not to any convent. She intended joining the community of which her aunt Margaret was prioress. Within a year Margaret died and her niece was elected in her place.

She lay with her cheek pressed against the damp and chilling floor and thought of her sons. Alexander, the eldest, was the only one who took after her. He had the elegant fair looks of the Hoppringles, whereas his father and brothers were darker and more heavily built. Would they all follow the King into England? she wondered.

The two youngest could not because they were not yet sixteen, but she was sure her husband would lead out the others.

When the service ended she sat up on her knees and rose to her feet, knowing that when she was old she would suffer badly from pains in her bones.

'Let that come,' she thought, 'for the moment there is enough to worry about.'

Nine

Duns was a prosperous, solid-looking old town with two long parallel main streets of fine stone buildings and narrow alleys running like the ribs of a fish between them. A large fortified castle guarded the town on its west side and the road to the east ran on towards Berwick on Tweed and the sea. It was famous for having produced a famous son, Duns Scotus, who had become a distinguished scholar at the University of Paris a couple of hundred years before.

As far as Lucy was concerned, it was the acme of sophistication, the biggest and most important place she had ever been in. Even Edinburgh or the English city of London couldn't be any grander than Duns, she thought.

She came into the town from the south because she'd taken to heart her mother's warning about the danger of meeting armed men, and travelled by old field tracks that she knew through accompanying her father on trips to deliver ground oats and barley to various farms. It took her and the plodding old grey most of the day to cover fifteen miles because she stopped often to allow the horse to crop grass and rest its legs. The sun shone all the time and she lay on her back on the grass beside the gentle old horse thinking about her brothers and the Hogg brothers. How unfair that they could ride off to war with their family weapons and loaded with food by their loving mothers when girls were left behind. She was sure she could wield a sword as well as any of them, certainly as well as poor Thomas anyway.

It was dusk when she rode along Duns' main street and reached her aunt's house at the corner of Gourlay's Loan. Holding the grey's reins in one hand, she rapped on the door with the other and a scared voice called out from the inside, 'Who's there? Go away.'

'It's me, Aunt Mary, it's Lucy from Sorley's Mill.'

The door swung open and her aunt stood inside with her arms thrown out in welcome. 'Lucy, what in Heaven's name are you doing here? Has your mother lost her senses? She never was very quick on the uptake, your mother.'

Thank goodness for that or I wouldn't be here, thought Lucy, but she stepped into her aunt's embrace and said, 'I've come to visit you. Thomas and Peter have mustered to join the King but girls aren't wanted and I thought I'd like to know where they're going.'

'Oh dear, so Peter and poor Thomas have been roped in. Your mother must be worried. But you shouldn't be here. It's not a place for women right now. The King's in town with all his court and people say no woman's safe anywhere near him.'

Lucy laughed. 'Now, now, Aunt Mary, don't talk so wild! Let me in or he might catch me.'

Mary reached out and grabbed her niece's arm. 'Come in, come in, leave your horse tied up there and I'll send a boy round to take it to the stable. Gourlay's working out the back because there's never been such a demand for mutton since he began working.'

Her husband, Peter Gourlay, was the eighth generation of his family to be fleshers in Duns. He was a cheerful, friendly man with a bright red face and a protuberant belly that gave a clue about his own partiality for good food. His wife adored him and he returned her feelings.

They were both delighted to entertain their youngest niece because the only cloud over their happy lives was their inability to have children.

As they piled food on her plate, Lucy was also given all the gossip about the tremendous excitement that was thrilling Duns. The King and his courtiers had ridden into town three days ago and set up their quarters in Duns Castle.

'They're very good for business,' said Gourlay, 'I've sold more mutton in three days than I've sold in the last year.'

His wife nodded and said, 'More great lords are coming to town every day and they all bring great crowds of servitors with them. They say the King's going to hold a parliament here. What an honour for our town.'

Lucy soaked up every word – the King and his nobles, parliaments and armies. What a good thing she decided to follow her brothers. Then, while her aunt and uncle were still talking animatedly, she laid her head down on the kitchen table and fell sound asleep.

Next morning she woke in a tiny attic room on the top floor of the house. Again the sun was shining and when she reached up to touch the ceiling above her head, it felt hot. Another fine day, a good harvest for her father. She stuck her head out of the narrow slit of a window and found herself looking down on a crowded street. People dressed in their best clothes were crowding along the roadway, jostling and pushing as if they were going somewhere very important.

Pulling a shawl over her shift, she shinned down the ladder that led downstairs and found her aunt in the kitchen making potted meat. 'What's happening outside?' she asked. 'There's crowds of people in the street.'

'It's the parliament. The King's holding it in a field at the edge of the town because there isn't a hall big enough for it in town. Get dressed and go along. There won't be a parliament held here ever again, I'm sure.'

'Don't you need help?' Lucy asked looking at the piles of chopped meat that covered the kitchen table.

'I'll manage. You go and tell me what you see when you get back.'

Barefoot and feeling insignificant in her home-woven skirt and blouse, the girl joined in the crowd flocking down the hill to a large meadow by the side of a stream. It was packed with people, some of whom were so tall that she could not see over their heads though she could hear the sound of drums and trumpets from somewhere in front of her. Suddenly she noticed that a crowd of small boys had shinned up tall oak trees at the side of the field. She'd always been good at climbing trees, better than her brothers. In a few seconds she'd tied her skirt between her legs and was up the tallest oak, from where she had a splendid view over the field.

She was straddling a large branch when the King rode into the throng from the south end. He looked so magnificent that the breath left her chest and she had to cling onto the branch with both hands to stop herself falling off. It was love at first sight.

'Oh, Aunt Mary,' she said later when she was back in Gourlay's Loan, 'he's so handsome. His hair is long and black but his beard is russet red. He has the finest face too and you know from the look of him that he is very clever and could make you laugh if he wanted to.'

'Charm the birds off the trees, you mean,' said Mary.

Lucy nodded. 'Yes. And his voice is deep and beautiful, like a singer's voice.' She was entranced with the King. In a strange way he reminded her of that rough man Lee from Redpath who had the same long dark hair and would look like James if he was dressed in fine robes and jewels instead of ragged shirts and leggings. For the first time she could understand what Ishbel saw in her lover.

'What did he say?' asked her aunt.

Lucy shook her head. 'I'm not sure. It was something about no lord who was killed in battle having to pay death dues.'

'His grand followers'd approve of that. They hate paying taxes,' said Mary.

'They certainly cheered. And he said he'd send a declaration of war by herald into England today.'

'Hmm, about time. If he isn't going to

make war, what is he going to do with all the fighting men that are camped out around our town? They're all eager to go now but they're gobbling up the provisions, and what'll happen when they've run out or are on their way back? I hope they take another road. Winners or losers.'

Mary sounded grim and Lucy said, 'But I thought you were pleased about the King being in Duns?'

'It's good now. They're all eating and drinking as if there's no tomorrow. Everybody in town is making money but on the way back they'll be stealing food, and if the English come, they'll be plundering and killing. I don't like wars, Lucy. I think you should get yourself back home before anything bad happens.'

The girl said nothing but she was sure of one thing. The last place she was going was home. What she had seen of the glory of the King's army had fired her imagination. If she could not fight with them, she could still follow. With the confidence of the young, she felt herself to be invincible. No matter what happened to others, she'd scrape through.

'But when I go back my mother will want to know news of the boys, especially Thomas,' she told her aunt.

'They're laddies, they'll take care of themselves. Anyway they won't be here in Duns. They're joining up with Lord Home, aren't they? The Borders men are mustering at Ellem Kirk and Bunkle Castle, the Home stronghold.'

Lucy looked crest fallen. 'How far away is that?'

'Bunkle's about six or seven miles north, near Preston. Ellem Kirk's near Longformacus, five miles or so. You're not to think about going there to find your brothers now. You'd get yourself killed or worse...'

'What a worrier Aunt Mary is,' thought Lucy, but she smiled and said, 'All right, don't worry. I'll go home, but I'll give the old horse another day to rest before I take the road again. Is that all right?'

'Of course it is. I'd keep you here with me always if I could, my dear, but you'd be safer at home.'

In the middle of the night Lucy woke and knew what she had to do. Creeping quietly down the ladder she took a pair of one of the apprentice's leather pants off a drying rack by the dying fire and searched for her aunt's silver scissors in a work basket. Putting them in her apron pocket, she gulped down some bread and buttermilk before going out to saddle up the grey. Pale streaks of light were appearing in the sky when she headed up the north track.

After three or four miles, she felt safe enough to stop and bundle her skirt round her waist as she pulled the pants up over her bare legs and feet. Then, pulling forward the long strands of her curling brown hair she hacked them off with the scissors till she could feel with her hands to make sure she had the sort of rough haircut boys had when they'd been afflicted by lice. Would she pass, she wondered. Her chest was still flat and her hips negligible. All she had to do was drop her voice a bit and remember to spit and swear. That should be easy.

Ten

Archibald Douglas, son of the trustworthy Earl of Angus, was a daring, fast rider so he was selected to carry confidential messages from the King to the Queen at Linlithgow.

Because he was not his father's eldest son, and therefore not heir to the estates or the ancient title, he was well aware that he would have to fend for himself as far as fortune was concerned. A good marriage to an heiress would suit him very well.

With that in view he frequented the court, ingratiating himself with everyone of importance, and because he was possessed both of good looks and considerable charm, he made many friends.

It did not take long for him to realize that the Queen was attracted to him. They were the same age and she was lonely, jealous of her husband's mistresses and sexually neglected though she was indulged by her husband in every other respect.

Neither he nor she was highly intelligent but they loved music, blithe conversation and, above all, gossip, so he made sure that he always had a titillating bit of news when he paid court to the Queen, which gradually became a daily event. His ambitions were kindled when he saw how her cheeks flushed and her eyes sparkled when he swept into her presence.

It did him no harm to pay court to her. Not only was he able to earn a privileged position at court where thanks to royal hospitality he could live for years on end without spending a groat, but there might be even greater rewards.

He'd heard his father talking about how the Stewarts were a short-lived family and how none of them died in their beds.

Now James was set on joining the English army in battle, and who knew what would be the outcome? It was even possible he would be killed, because he was not the sort of man to stay out of the middle of a fight. Archibald's father often spoke with regret about the King's reckless and impulsive nature.

When the King and his army reached Duns, Archibald was despatched with a letter for the Queen. It was closed with the royal seal so he could not sneak a look at it, but he stood at her side when she read it and knew what it said before she did.

Stricken-faced, she looked up at him. 'My husband says that I have to go to Holyrood as soon as possible and wait for him there.'

'His Majesty must want to see you before he marches into England,' he said soothingly.

'But what about my son? I can't take him to Edinburgh. The plague is still raging there.' She looked genuinely terrified of the danger.

Douglas bent down over her shoulder and put his finger on the last line of the letter. 'It says you must leave the baby in Linlithgow. The King is mindful of the dangers of the plague as well as you are.'

'Must I leave him?' she asked for she went nowhere without the precious baby and watched over him every hour of the day.

The ladies of her chamber rushed up to crowd round and reassure her. 'The Prince will be safe, Your Highness. We'll watch over him. You must go because the King wants to take his farewell of you.'

The Fleming woman, who could not hide the amused malice in her eyes, added, 'And if you stay all the time in bed in your chamber at the Palace, madam, there will be no chance of you being infected by the plague. It's dying out anyway.'

Margaret stared at her as realization dawned. *Stay in bed in your chamber* ... That was why he was sending for her. He intended to make her pregnant again. They had not slept together since she fell pregnant with their son, who was now almost a year and a half old.

Conjugal relations had been suspended after the birth as well because she was ill for many months and was only now recovering but last week her personal physician, who her husband had brought over from Spain, advised that she was well enough to have another child.

James must know that. He was always very concerned about her health and also deeply interested in medicine. He often went to watch Edinburgh's best surgeons performing operations and also tried his hand at dentistry, which particularly interested him. More than once he told her that if he was not a king, he would like to have trained as a medical man.

Now she was recovered, she would be expected to go through the ordeal of childbirth again. She wondered which of her women had been informing the King about the details of her health and menstrual cycle, for in two days she would be at her most fertile.

That was why she was being ordered to Holyrood like a brood mare.

Part of her rebelled at the prospect.

What if I refuse to go? she wondered.

But she was afraid of James, who could display fearsome outbreaks of violence and temper. His father, after all, was said to have murdered his mother.

There was no avoiding it. She would have to go and she knew why. James was going to war and, of course, was well aware of the chance of being killed. To ensure the continuity of the Stewart line, it would be better to have two legitimate sons instead of only one.

Turning towards the Fleming woman, who she suspected was the spy, she said crisply, 'Pack my boxes but not with much. I will not be away from my son for long,' and turned on her heel, knowing that giggling would break out behind her as soon as she left the room.

Douglas, the royal messenger, took upon himself to be commander of the guard of honour that escorted Margaret on her journey to Edinburgh. For speed and safety she rejected the chance to travel in a litter and instead rode pillion behind him with her arm round his waist.

She was already thrilled at the prospect of making love again after so long and every nerve was tingling with anticipation as she pressed herself against Douglas's back. The proximity of a male body gave her a deep visceral thrill for he was slim and taut-muscled.

After a while, pretending to doze, she leant her head against him and felt the sinews of his back tighten. Breathing in deeply she savoured his smell – and it made her stomach churn with the visceral energy flowing between them.

He wants me as much as I want him, she thought with delight.

Though she was a woman of strong desires, she had never taken a lover because of her fear of James' vengeance. He had to be sure that her children were fathered by him and no one else. If he doubted that, there was no knowing what he might do. After all, he certainly conspired in the murder of his father. He admitted that himself and always wore an iron chain around his waist as a penitential act of self-chastisement. He did not even take it off in bed – and it hurt her when they slept together. She always wondered if he took it off with the Fleming woman.

There were even rumours that it was James, and not Elphinstone or her father, who organized the poisoning of Margaret Drummond and her sisters.

She was absorbed in those thoughts when

a strand of Douglas's soft curly hair blew back in her face and tickled her cheek. She wanted to reach up and stroke his head but instead let one of her hands linger on his neck as she brushed the hair away. By the way he stiffened, she knew that he felt the mysterious surging power between them, and enjoyed it. For the first time in her life she was possessed of sexual power and revelled in it, taking more and more risks with her wandering hands in his hair till they finally arrived at Holyrood, where she dismounted with regret.

As her feet touched the ground, she held out a hand to him and demurely thanked him for her safe journey. He kissed the cuff of her glove and said in a low voice, 'It was a pleasure to serve Your Majesty.' His imagination – and ambitions – had been greatly stimulated by the journey.

I'm a desirable woman, a woman that men admire, she thought joyfully as she walked into the vast hall of the palace with all her hormones raging.

She was still burning with desire and anticipation when James came to her chamber that night after riding as if the Devil was after him from the encampment at Ellem Kirk thirty miles away.

He himself had been surprised by the sudden impulse that came upon him to father another child. In the middle of one night at Duns Castle he'd woken with the terrifying conviction that he was going to die soon.

No matter how much he rationalized the fear, it did not go away. How much happier he would be if he knew that his crown would pass to his eldest illegitimate son, Alexander, dear Meg's boy, who had great spirit and looked so like her. But that was not possible; though he had gone through a hand-fasting ceremony with Meg their marriage was never officially accepted. Such a ceremony would have been legal for any subject in his kingdom but it could be set aside for kings.

He had been adamant not to consider any other alliance, especially the Tudor one, when she was alive and so he was convinced that his stubbornness had brought about her untimely death. He was convinced that she was killed to clear the way for his marriage with Henry VII's daughter ten years ago and the signing of the facilely named Treaty of Perpetual Peace that took place at the same time.

He remembered his anguish as he stood in Dunkeld Cathedral watching the funeral services of Margaret and her two sisters – for they had all died together after dining at the same table.

He'd scanned the faces around him and wondered who was responsible. The cathedral was packed with Scotland's nobility, many of whom had their own reasons for keeping the Drummonds away from power. Others were in the pay of the English, or looking for advancement through them.

'Was it you? Was it you?' he asked himself as he scanned the downcast faces around him. He was forever after plagued by suspicion, even of Bishop Elphinstone, who had been the man he admired most when he was growing up.

Alexander, his twenty-two-year-old son delighted him because he was suave, handsome and devil-may-care – the sort of young man James had been himself.

Like his father, he had a fiery temper and tended to act without thinking but those were faults his father overlooked because he shared them. When they spent time together, paternal pride filled James and he would have given half of his possessions to be able to pass the throne onto the boy but bastardy made that impossible.

Every time one of his legitimate sons sickened and died, he felt that he was being punished by God for conniving with the rebels who killed his father, even though the man was as wicked as the Devil.

The last boy was living at least but there was always the fear that some congenital weakness might prevent him reaching adulthood. A second-string heir had to be provided.

His wife was not good at having healthy children. She did not carry them well. All her babies except the last died before their first birthdays, sometimes before the end of their first week.

It was dangerous to rely on one. Before it was too late he must impregnate Margaret again. So he sent Douglas to summon her to Holyrood, which was closer for him than Linlithgow.

With a small party of only three men he rode through the night with his head full of memories of other journeys he'd undertaken for love. This one had the same purpose – to bed a woman – but it was very different as far as anticipating enjoyment was concerned.

It was nearly dawn when he arrived at the Palace and mounted the great staircase at a run. Margaret was asleep in bed when he flung the door of her chamber open, taking off his cloak at the same time. She sat up and gasped at the sight.

Though it was less than ten days since she'd seen him, he had changed. There was something demonic about him now that scared her.

'My lord...' she stammered and held out her hand for him to kiss but he swept it aside.

'Help me pull off my boots,' he ordered, sitting on the edge of the bed and sticking out a leg. She did as she was told and stood shivering in the middle of the floor watching as he pulled his clothes over his head. She had never seen him in such a frenzy before. When the last piece of clothing fell to the floor, he was naked except for the belt of metal chains round his waist. With a gesture he told her to get into the bed and fell in beside her, pulling up her nightshirt.

'Lie still!' he commanded as he entered her without any preamble. She groaned, 'James, James, that chain hurts me. Please take it off.'

He ignored her and went plunging on till he climaxed. Then he fell back, turned over and prepared to go to sleep.

For the first time in their marriage she protested, digging him in the back with her elbow and saying, 'Didn't you hear me asking you to take off that chain? It cuts into my flesh.'

He turned back and eyed her coldly. 'I take it off for nobody.'

'My women tell me you took it off for Margaret Drummond,' she snapped back. It was the first time his mistress's name had been mentioned between them.

He did not deny it. 'Only for her because it hurt her but for no one else. Ever.'

'But I am your wife and it hurts me.'

He shut his eyes. 'Ours is but a dynastic alliance. Go to sleep.'

She lay with tears sliding down her cheeks

for a long time. Never before had he been so discourteous, for his treatment of her had always been courtly and polite, and their lovemaking cursory, but not brutal like tonight's frenzy. Tonight she knew that not only did he not love her, he did not like her either.

As she fell asleep she thought about her doting dead father. How could he have been so unthinking as to marry his favourite daughter to this man? Of course she knew that considerations of romantic love did not enter into royal marriages, but affection could grow, as it had done between her parents, whose marriage had been arranged to unite the houses of York and Lancaster. Hers was to unite England and Scotland but it had failed in every respect, political as well as sexual.

James was determined to leave nothing to chance, and mounted her in the same perfunctory way when he woke in the morning. As he left he told her to expect him that evening as well. Never in ten years of marriage had he mated with her so often in such a short period of time but it was a purely functional exercise. When he left on the second morning, they took formal leave of each other. She wondered if she would ever see him again but knew, deeply and instinctively, that he had planted another child in her womb.

Eleven

The weather was spectacularly fine and the corn was ripening in the fields by mid-August when groups of men began converging on Duns from all over the south of Scotland. On their way they met up with each other and exchanged news.

'Duns is closed to armed men now because it's brim full. Home's men have to muster at Ellem Kirk above Longformacus,' a group of men from Greenlaw told the contingent from Melrose, Dryburgh and the Leader valley when they met up near the town.

'It's bonny up there at Ellem Kirk,' said cheerful Sandy Hogg, and Sam Lee looked at him as if he'd taken leave of his senses. 'Who cares if it's bonny? We're off to war, lad, and there's naething bonny about that.'

But Sandy was right. It was bonny. Long green valleys ran between rounded hills covered with thick scrub of oak, sloes, hawthorn and rowan trees. Purple fruit hung like jewels on the branches of the sloes and made a striking contrast with the scarlet of rose-hips and rowans. Ellem Kirk, a tiny chapel, stood on a little hill above the fast flowing Whiteadder River where fish jumped in the sparkling sunshine. More than one man got down off his horse and waded into the water with his hands cupped to guddle for trout, which would make a welcome addition to his supper.

Retainers of Lord Home, their feudal superior, rode to and fro surveying new arrivals and directing them to bivouac in various wooded coverts or grassy meadows. All they were interested in was where were they from, how many men were in their group, were they well armed, what with, and did they have enough food?

Sam Lee took over the command of his brothers and his immediate neighbours, the Purvises and the Hoggs. 'Stay with me and I'll see you're safe,' he told them, and, overwhelmed by the vast crowd around them, they did as they were told.

Sam went off to find out information and came back with the news that they were to follow Home to Coldstream, where they would be able to cross the Tweed into England. Because of the fine summer, the river would be low and very fordable.

His younger followers gasped in anticipation. None of them had seriously expected ever to set foot on English soil.

'The King's been here, but he's gone back to Holyrood. He'll be returning with the big cannons from Edinburgh Castle to blast the walls of Norham Castle. I hope we don't miss that,' said Sam. He would be bitterly disappointed to miss besieging Norham because his aim in going to war was to gather as much plunder as possible and there should be plenty of it there for the castle belonged to the Bishop of Durham and was rumoured to be richly furnished.

Perhaps, he thought, a chance would come to load himself up with valuables and make his way home before any serious fighting started. Following Home's men into war was not a very good idea because in their number were many Border rievers and thieves like himself. To be in the front and without rivals in the looting business, it would be better to leave Home's men and attach himself to the King's contingent because many of the men marching with him were townspeople like the burgesses of Edinburgh and Glasgow who did not want to fight and were only interested in serving their time and going home again.

While he was striding about, gathering news, mixing with armed men from all over the countryside, Sam attracted attention. He was handsome and bold and appeared unimpressed by title, so other men stared at him and wondered who he was. In his wanderings he was spotted by a Home retainer, who rode up to him and asked, 'Who are you? Where are you from?'

'Who are you?'

'I'm Lord Home's man and don't you sharp-tongue me or I'll run you through. Who are you and why are you here?'

'I'm not a tenant of Home, if that's what you're asking. My name is Lee and my place is at Redpath, near Earlston, and it's Dryburgh Abbey land.'

The man on the horse leaned over and poked Sam in the ribs with the shaft of his pike. 'I don't care who you pay your rent to, if you do pay your rent. Come with me. My lord wants to see you.'

Lord Home was surveying his gathering army from the saddle of a huge war horse and when his man brought Sam up to him, he looked round, laughed, took a second look and then laughed again.

'Well done. That's him. Where did you find him?' he asked the retainer.

'In the mob. You're right. He's good, isn't he?'

'He's perfect. I thought so when I caught a glimpse of him swaggering about this morning. He's almost a double except for the beard.'

And to Sam he said, 'How long does it take your beard to grow?'

'Quite quick. I have to shave often to keep it down.'

'What colour is it?' asked Home.

'What colour do you think?' retorted Sam, holding up a strand of his long hair. He thought the wizened-looking man on the white horse was mad.

'I can see it's black but has it a red tint when it grows?'

'A bit, I suppose.'

'You'll do,' said Home and turned to his henchman again, saying, 'Get him a war horse and some proper clothes and he can ride with me.'

Even arrogant Sam was confused by what was going on and looked from face to face with his eyebrows raised. 'What are you up to?' he asked but Home didn't answer. It was the retainer who spoke.

'From the distance you're his double. The King's double, I mean. You'll be useful to confuse people, especially spies. But remember, keep your mouth shut. Anybody who hears that Border drawl won't be taken in.'

It was hard for Sam to hide his jubilation. To ride about dressed like the King and have people bending the knee to him was like being in a dream. He went with Home's man like a biddable child, completely forgetting about his brothers and the others he'd left behind him camped on the side of the hill.

When Sam did not come back, the Lee brothers had a whispered discussion. From what they'd overheard among others in the crowd that was growing every day, already some men were quietly disappearing and making their way home again.

There was always an excuse – the most frequent one was that the harvest needed gathering in and there no one at home to do it.

The absentees had done their duty, after all. They turned up, counted in and nobody after that would miss them in the mass of forced volunteers that milled around apparently unsupervised except by the men who marched in with them.

Neither patriotism nor duties at home meant anything to men like the Lees, their only lure was plunder. Sam's brothers knew he was not likely to decamp before there was a chance of helping himself to something more valuable than a horse. He could steal one of those any day.

'He's on the trail of something good. We'd better stay around till he comes back with it,' said Sam's squint-eyed eldest brother.

'I'm not for getting myself killed while I wait,' said the youngest brother. 'There'll only be women and no fighting men left back at home. I could steal a few good horses if I was back there, I'm sure.'

The others agreed, so it was decided that one brother, the youngest, should slip away when darkness fell and the other two would wait for Sam's return. They shook hands on the bargain that anything valuable any of them collected would be shared with his brothers, and in the morning only two Lees marched on with the rabble army.

Getting to Ellem Kirk was a harder task than Lucy imagined when she set off from Duns. Though the distance was only five miles, the paths by which she travelled took her over scrubland and through marshes. At one point, stopping to lead the grey over a stony stream, she twisted her ankle and hopped about in agony for a few minutes before she was able to climb back on the horse's back only to find that it was limping too.

After three hours, when she was beginning to panic about being lost, she gazed out from a rise in the land and saw in the valley below groups of armed men who were travelling in the same direction. 'It's all right. We're not lost after all,' she exulted to the old horse as she laid her face alongside its neck.

At last, well after midday, they limped up another long hill and stopped on the top to stare down into a valley through which ran a river which she guessed was the Whiteadder. If she was right, she'd reached her destination, for Ellem Kirk was built on its banks. Her eyesight was good and as she stared and stared she was able to make out a mass of men milling about like ants in front of an anthill on the grassy fields alongside the shining river.

There were so many of them it was impossible to even consider counting or even estimating their number and she realized with a sinking heart how difficult it would be to find her brothers or Sandy Hogg in such a crowd. Dropping her hands onto the pommel she almost despaired, wondering if she should give up and go home as she had told Aunt Mary she intended to do.

But that would be cowardly, as if she was running away, when she was only on the brink of her big adventure and there was little enough adventure in most women's lives as far as she could see. Aunt Mary and her mother were happy with their cooking and gossiping but nothing ever happened to them that was not organized by men. Lucy wanted to be different and perhaps this was her only chance.

Sitting on her old grey horse on the top of the hill, she considered her options. Go home on a limping horse and face her father's reprimands? Go home and endure Peter, Thomas and Sandy talking about following the King for the rest of her life? She was so close ... In the field below was a vast army, probably the King himself was there, that glorious man she'd seen at Duns!

'I'll go. I'll go!' she told the horse as she sat down firmly in the saddle and stuck her heels into its sides. In the guise of a boy, she was going to tag on at the end of the throng.

Reluctantly the grey staggered down the hill. It was obviously on its last legs and she felt pity for it. 'Go on, go on,' she urged, 'I'll find you a fine field of grass down there,' and as if it understood her, it plodded on. One or two men glanced at her as rode into the verges of the crowd and one grey-bearded man asked, 'Looking for somebody in particular, lad?'

Good, he thought she was a boy. Her deception must be working.

'No,' she growled, 'I'm wanting to join up and fight the English.'

The man was kind-looking. He laughed and said, 'Ye're awfy keen. Aren't ye a bit young for fighting? They don't take bairns under sixteen. War isn't a game. Go back home and stay alive for a bit longer. Where have ye come from, onywey?'

Lucy stared defiantly at him, pointed to the west and said, 'I am sixteen and I've come from over that hill.'

The old man laughed, 'Och, ye're just a daft laddie. I was like that when I was young. But you haven't even got a sword. Come on, tell me your real age.'

'*Sixteen!*' It was an effort to make her voice rough enough.

'Huh, not yet if you ask me. But you're determined to go, aren't you? I'm no' for seeing laddies getting themselves killed before their time, though. Come wi' me and I'll find you a safe place.' The old man's eyes were concerned.

Lucy jumped off the horse and followed his beckoning hand. He looked sceptically at her limping gait and said, 'You're going short, aren't ye? Ye wouldnae even be able to run away if the English came.'

He led her up to a huge ox cart that was piled high with sacks of provisions and guarded by two men with swords at their waists. One of them was a grizzled veteran like Lucy's protector, who said to her, 'This man here is my friend Willie White from Kelsae. We've fought in many battles together, but now we're in charge of food carts. It's safer than running into a pitched battle at our age. You can help Willie because you don't need a dagger in your belt to serve men with bread and mutton stew. He'll look after ye and when you get home again remember to tell your mother that Tom Taylor from Selkirk saved your life.'

The man he called Willie White grinned, showing broken yellow teeth. 'He's an old blether. What's he telling you to do?' he said to Lucy.

'I'm telling him he's going to be your helper. He can do your running aboot for ye because those legs of yours arenae up tae much these days, are they?'

Willie agreed, sticking out a bandaged leg.

'I could do with a handy laddie,' he agreed.

'Well, now you've got one and he's got a bad leg too, so that makes twae guid legs between the pair of ye,' said Tom, pointing at Lucy.

'There's no' much of ye, is there, so you won't need a lot of feeding,' said Willie. 'I need a laddie to pluck chickens and build fires. The yin I brought wi' me was greetin' for his mother and I sent him hame. Could you do his work? And what's your name, anyway?' he asked.

She'd helped her mother do both those things often enough so she nodded as she cudgelled her mind for a suitable name. Nothing came to mind. 'What do we call you?' asked Willie again.

'Call me Hoppy,' she said, thinking of her painful ankle and a lame boy she knew at home who was called that.

White laughed. 'Because you're short in the leg? Right then, hop up onto my wagon and come along with me but I canna take that old horse of yours along too because it's lame and we can't spare the fodder for it. Turn it into one of the fields and let it take its chance.'

Lucy remounted and rode the grey up a track past the little chapel to a green clearing and slipped off its bridle and saddle. The summer grass was trodden down but it would be lush again as soon as this crowd moved on so the horse wouldn't starve and when she got the chance she'd try to send word to tell her uncle where to collect it.

'Goodbye, old friend,' she said as she clapped it on the neck for the last time.

She was sitting high on the top of sacks of flour in the Kelso cart as it trundled along when Lord Home came round to make his inspection of the fodder train. Her cropped head was covered with an old bonnet that she'd found discarded along the way, and round her shoulders she was clutching a black and white shepherd's plaid that kind Tom Taylor had procured for her. 'For a laddie that's so determined to go to war, you haven't come out very well equipped,' he said.

The earl was an insignificant-looking skinny fellow but the men of his entourage were glorious in bright coloured tabards over armour and burnished steel bonnets. Riding by the earl's side, however, was an even prouder figure that made people in the crowd gape, for he was dark-haired, richly dressed, proud of nose and arrogant of eye. Was it the King, they whispered to each other.

Could it be? He hadn't been seen for two days. Was he back now to rally them on their way? But if it was him, wouldn't he be riding in front of Home and not behind him? But there was such a likeness and such obvious arrogant pride...

Lucy, as bedazzled as everyone else, stared at this magnificent personage and caught his glance. Something flashed in his eye and immediately she knew him. In spite of her hair cut and black bonnet, he recognized her too. It was not the King, it was Sam Lee! What was he doing dressed up like a lord in the entourage of the Earl of Home? The look that passed between them warned, 'You say nothing and I'll do the same.'

Twelve

Everybody in the little town of Coldstream, except those who were too ill or infirm to leave their homes, turned out at dawn on the morning of 22nd August to watch King James and his army cross the Tweed and invade England. It was an awe-inspiring sight.

First came the cannons under the marshal-ship of Robert Borthwick, a seasoned war-rior who rode up and down the lines of heaving men and oxen yelling and cracking a whip over shoulders of men and animals alike.

He had under his command ordnance that was greater than anything the English would be able to muster and though he had left the famous Mons Meg cannon at home in Edinburgh Castle, he still had forty huge guns and a dazzling collection of twelve brass cannons that glittered in the morning sunshine. In spite of having been on the road for the best part of a month, these cannons were kept polished, gleaming and dangerous-looking.

You could not say the same for the lines of men that hauled them along. Many of them were criminals, saved from the gallows in return for this brute labour. They were sweaty and filthy, bowed down with their burdens, scowling and swearing like demons.

The King rode up to Borthwick when the first party stopped on the edge of the river and said, 'It's a blessing that the weather continues fair and the river's running low.'

The cannonry master frowned. 'There was a scarlet dawn this morning and that's a bad sign. The locals say that rain is coming. They've had fair weather for too long and the clouds are gathering in the north.'

James waved a gloved hand. 'Then get as much over as you can before it comes. Start with the heaviest ordnance before the river bed breaks up.'

'It's a good ford. I've parties of labourers waiting to lay straw bales on the bed if it does start breaking. We'll get everything over, Your Majesty. Don't worry.'

He sounded more confident than he felt because even in good conditions getting such a vast army over the broad river would be a slow job. He turned in his saddle and saw behind him line after line of mounted and walking men building up along the river's northern bank, and more were arriving all the time.

James did not share his cannon master's apprehensions for he rode off jubilant, confident that Borthwick would manage the immense task. He was the best in his field in the whole of Europe. Like Borthwick, James looked back at the gathering men behind him and felt an immense surge of pride. Never before had Scotland summoned up such an army. It was invincible. He laughed out loud and swung one arm up in the air as he imagined himself marching triumphant through Northumberland – perhaps even besieging London. Nothing was impossible.

The knights and nobles who always gathered round him caught the infection of his high spirits and raised a cheer, though not all of them were as set on the enterprise as he was.

Exuberant as a drunk man, he gazed across

the river to the reedy banks on the other side and, pointing a hand on which four glittering rings flashed and shone, shouted, 'There's England! Look at the trees, look at the hills, look at the houses. Soon they'll all be mine.'

The Earl of Douglas, one of the courtiers who had misgivings about the invasion they were about to undertake, grunted, 'There'll be a battle to fight first, sire.'

The King stared back, his eyes suddenly hard, and said, 'You're as bad as Elphinstone. God is on my side, Douglas.'

In preparation for this huge enterprise, he had risen very early in Duns Castle to be shriven by his favourite priest and say prayers to his own special protector, St Ninian. He wished he'd had the time to go on pilgrimage to Ninian's shrine at Whithorn but it was too distant, five hard days' journey away on the other side of Scotland, and it would be a mistake to give Henry time to send more troops back to England from France. However, he vowed to Ninian that Whithorn would be the first place he'd head for after he returned victorious from England. Praying to Ninian had driven away any gloomy forebodings that might otherwise have plagued his mind.

He suddenly became aware that a group of black-clad women were standing in the wide gateway of Coldstream Abbey on the rise of ground that overlooked the ford. They were the nuns of the order that lived there.

He knew Isabella Hoppringle, the abbess, because she had often attended court with her husband Wedderburn before she took the veil. Even from a distance James recognized her in the group because she was the tallest, the thinnest and the most elegantly intimidating.

She'd always been a serious-minded, critical woman, unfortunately rather humourless, and he did not blame her husband for taking his pleasures with others of easier temperaments. Nevertheless she must be treated with deference because she was a powerful figure, with contacts on both sides of the border, and it was best to stay in her good graces. Rumour had it that she would not draw back from giving information to or collaborating with the enemy if it suited her purpose.

He rode up to the abbey gate and gave her a fulsome salute, which she returned with a deep curtsy, and a fervent blessing, her dark skirt sweeping in the dust. 'May God preserve you, my lord and King. I pray that He will keep you safe.' She spoke humbly but her eyes seemed to be summing him up and he felt he was found wanting.

Suddenly he felt vulnerable. Was the woman a witch? Did she see things that ordinary mortals did not?

She was speaking again. 'We have prepared food and drink for you. Please come in and honour us with your presence.'

He looked over his shoulder at the men closest to him, his son Alexander and the earls of Lennox and Douglas, who were all smiling at the prospect of eating in the abbey, for the abbess's hospitality was famed.

'Thank you,' said the King. 'We will be honoured.'

A group of eight men who were closest to the King dismounted and walked behind him into the quiet green cloister. Somewhere above their heads a bell tolled eight o'clock and a flutter of white doves flew up into the air.

The old Earl of Douglas, who had come through many campaigns and was very apprehensive about the outcome of this one, stared around deeply comforted by the atmosphere of peace and serenity.

As the last notes of the bell died away a silent prayer was running through his head. 'Preserve my sons, O God, and preserve me too but that's not as important as protecting my boys.' Behind him in the throng outside the gate were four of his sons and he was apprehensive about them. So apprehensive that he had organized the role of messenger for Alexander to stay at home so that he would not be involved in any hand-to-hand fighting, if it came to that. At least one

Douglas had to survive if there was a terrible defeat.

He was not a coward and was not sure why he felt so uneasy. Perhaps it was because he felt this war of Jamie's was contrived and unprovoked. It was not an act of chivalry to attack an enemy in the back while he was fighting another foe. His advice to ignore the petty difficulties about the Queen's dowry had been ignored by the King, who was determined to fight.

Walking along beside the abbess, the King was being his most charming, especially complimenting her on the tranquillity and comfort of the abbey's buildings.

'My aunt who was head of the house before me organized it and it has always been so,' she said.

'You are too modest. I know you play an important role in diplomatic affairs because you are perched on the border between two warring countries. Your abbey must have trodden a dangerous line on many occasions. Look how often other Border abbeys have been sacked, but it has always stayed secure,' he said.

She avoided returning his glance because she knew he was hinting that she was suspected of running with the hare and hunting with the hounds, channelling information and providing hospitality for Scots and English alike. He could think what he liked!

How else did he expect her abbey to survive?

'We are too poor and insignificant to attract much attention,' she said, though she was well aware that her money chest and granaries were as full as, if not fuller than, any other religious establishment in the south of Scotland. That was her pride and achievement.

As she showed James into the refectory she could not help admiring his tall figure and proud demeanour. Though she was a nun she was not impervious to the attraction of a handsome man. Wedderburn had been handsome too when she married him, but he turned out to be brutal and hard. This one was not. If anything he was too sensitive and romantic and she admired his ranging mind. A musician, an artist, a seeker after knowledge.

Elphinstone with whom she exchanged letters had told her of James' desire to dabble in medicine, an area of knowledge that attracted her too. She wished she was able to talk to him about how he'd learned to pull teeth without causing too much agony to the patient but that was not the sort of topic that was suitable for discussing over a meal.

What a pity, she thought, that he had been born to sit on a throne and was not able to direct his talents into a narrower and perhaps more fulfilling field – certainly a safer one, because the Stewart kings had always been beset by enemies, both abroad and at home.

Though she was prepared to go to any lengths and deal with anybody for the good of her abbey, she was a fervent lover of Scotland, as patriotic as anyone, but she was not going to allow her heart to rule her head. Not like poor James, who, she suspected, had been ruled by his emotions throughout his life. She hoped they would not lead him to disaster. People said he scourged himself because he'd looked the other way when his father was being punished for his crimes, and she'd heard talk of the penitential iron chain he wore around his waist as an act of atonement for involvement in his father's murder. Not that he'd done the killing, but it was done by older men who then put him on the throne at the age of fifteen – a child.

James III deserved what he got, in her opinion, because he had been universally despised as a venal, cruel pederast, and was suspected of killing his wife, Margaret of Denmark, this king's mother.

Her surge of sympathetic understanding for the man beside her at the table made her smile at the King with genuine and not assumed sympathy and he saw the change come over her. He knew he had gone up in her regard.

'Have you news of your husband and sons, my lady?' he asked, for he'd first met her when she attended his court as the wife of a nobleman.

'I believe they're following you to war, my lord. I expect to entertain them here with other members of my family when they cross the Tweed after you,' she said.

In fact she had posted men at the ford to intercept her sons and bring them into the abbey to receive her blessing.

Apart from entertaining the King and his inner circle, the demands on her abbey's hospitality would be large from her family alone today because she was born a Hoppringle, an important family with powerful connections and lands all the way up the Tweed valley. Her favourite uncle was the Laird of Torwoodlee, whose lands spread out along the Gala water and up to Soutra Hospital on the ridge of hills overlooking Edinburgh. He and his sons would also certainly be following their king into England.

James ate little from her loaded table, drank one cup of mead, then took his leave, striding back to the abbey gate where he mounted his war horse and splashed across the waters of the ford into England. As she stood on the grassy bank watching him go, she wondered if she would ever see him again.

At that moment a dark cloud passed over the morning sun and she shivered. A change was coming over the weather. It was a good thing they were crossing the river today and had not waited till tomorrow for by then it would surely rain, and when it rained the ford was treacherous.

She did not have enough time to walk back to the cloisters before she saw the Wedderburn banner flying on the bank of the river among the lines of men waiting to cross the ford. Pointing it out to a man watching beside her, she said, 'That's my husband's banner. Go and fetch my sons to me. I want to bless them.'

When they rode up she was standing at the main door of the abbey church with her hands folded. Her heart began racing as she saw her magnificent young men walking towards her. Though she knew pride was sinful, she could not help it rising inside her.

They were five handsome men – the two youngest had been left behind because they were not yet sixteen. She had given birth to them all. She had given them the gift of life and now they were tall and proud, towering over lesser men around them like pagan gods. The most handsome was her beautiful eldest son, Alexander, who looked like her own father, the best looking of them all, but they were all her sons and she loved them. Tears pricked her eyes as they walked towards her but she blinked them back and held out her hands in blessing.

'God preserve you all. I am glad you are

doing your duty by your native land,' she said in a calm voice.

One by one they knelt down in front of her without speaking, some of them grim-faced because they resented the fact she had chosen the religious life instead of staying with her family.

With gentle hands she touched the top of each head, murmuring their names as she did so, but sensed there was little sympathy from any of them, except the first, who raised his eyes to her when she gave him his blessing.

When she left the boys' father, they felt she had abandoned them, and they were more in sympathy with him anyway, interested in masculine things like hunting and fighting but not in praying or worshipping God. They disregarded the fact that she might have had other reasons to want to be free of the marriage.

She did not ask if Wedderburn was with them, or if he intended to meet her, because she knew that neither he nor she had any wish to see each other again.

They stayed only a few moments and when she watched them walk away again a few tears did flow unchecked but only the nun by her side saw them.

Rain began to fall heavily in mid-afternoon, but men kept marching through the ford, and she stood under the gatehouse arch watching them. Never in her imagination could she have guessed that James would gather such a vast number.

Even after darkness fell, on and on they streamed, small and tall, mounted and on foot, well armed or apparently defenceless, some even without the protection of a small shield. There were Highlanders in tattered plaids; drilled soldiers in shining armour marching in strict array; rich men mounted on fine horses; poor men on foot, some already limping.

How many of this host will come back again? she wondered as she watched.

Thirteen

To realize that they were standing with English soil beneath their boots was sobering for the men of the Scottish army. It was no longer a jaunt or a diversion from everyday life. They were well and truly launched on a vast and serious enterprise. There was no turning back. It had to end in fighting

Everybody knew that by marching into

England, James had utterly broken the Treaty of Perpetual Peace signed at the time of his marriage to Margaret. He was the aggressor, so by the laws of diplomacy he was in the wrong. Even the intercessions of the wily French King Louis XII, who had lured and flattered him into this war, would not win him a sanction from the Pope for the enterprise.

Marching with Lord Home's men, the group from Selkirk crossed the ford just after midday and marched on for a couple of miles till they reached the narrow, hump-backed Twizel Bridge that crossed the little River Till before it ran down from England into the Tweed. The walls of Twizel Castle rose above their heads on top of the cliff but there was absolutely no activity to be seen inside it. No flag flew and there were no guards on the gate.

Even the boldest men among the Scots looked up at the castle and wondered if it was safe to attack it. It looked deserted but perhaps that was a trap.

The bridge arched over a deep and narrow part of the river and they decided to wait for orders, sheltering from the driving rain beneath the bridge and gloomily surveying their prospects.

'So this is England?' one man said.

'It doesnae look much different to home,' said another.

'Perhaps Edward was right to stay in Selkirk,' grumbled Dan Fletcher as he emptied water out of his top boots.

His brother Robert turned on him like an angry dog.

'Don't let me hear you saying his name again. He's a yellow-livered coward and a disgrace to our name. The Fletchers have lived in Selkirk for hundreds of years and never failed in their duty to the King before.'

'All right, all right,' said Dan pacifically, 'we're all here now, aren't we?'

'And going on, not like some of the scum that are slipping away already,' said Robert.

They had noticed that several of the Borders contingent had quietly taken to their heels before any serious fighting began. 'They crossed to England, didn't they? They won't be missed, not in such a huge army, one or two less won't make much difference,' said Dan, who was beginning to think Edward was the most sensible one among them.

'It's a matter of honour and obligation,' retorted his brother but Dan's only answer was a snort.

Amongst the men from Melrose and Dryburgh, who were camped nearby, there were also some others who longed to return home but the two abbots had included in their levy a group of muscular brothers who marshalled their forces and took note of anybody who ran away.

Explanations would be demanded when all the trouble was over for they were only tenants after all and their rent included the obligation of providing fighting men when necessary. So even malcontents muttered among themselves but kept on marching though they were counting the remaining days of their obligation.

The Lee brothers did not seem to be afflicted with battle apprehension. They chaffed the others, particularly the young Hoggs and the two Purvis boys. 'What are you still doing here? You should take off before you get your throats cut,' they said.

Peter Purvis angrily retorted, 'So why are you staying? Why don't you take off like your brother?' There had been no sign of Sam for days.

'We're only here till we fill our saddle bags. If all you laddies run away home now there'll be more for us to gather in.'

'I'm no' runnin' awa'. I saw the King yesterday and he's a braw callant,' said Thomas Purvis staunchly.

The oldest Lee laughed. 'It takes a daftie to admire a daftie, if you ask me.'

Lucy, unaware that her brothers were camped less than half a mile away, limped around the food wagons carrying pans of oatmeal skirlie and hard bread to disgruntled men crowding round and hungry for food. 'Is this all you've got? Where's the meat? Men canna fight on skirlie,' they groaned.

'Ye're not fighting yet,' she snapped, 'and it's too wet for our fires to burn. We've got meat but we canna roast it.'

'Give me a haunch of mutton and I'll eat it raw,' said one giant whose job at home was to carry buckets of water from the town well to the houses around Kelso square.

Fortunately there was plenty of ale and by the time Lucy had distributed enough of it, the grumbling stopped and the singing began.

Tired out, she climbed onto the largest cart and hid herself among half-open sacks, pulling some over herself so that she was out of sight. Willie had told her to do that as well as providing her with a wooden-handled carving knife and the advice to stick it straight into anyone who tried to 'bother' her. Sometimes she was afraid that he guessed her secret, for he often looked at her with a strange expression in his eyes, but he asked no questions and he and old Tom had set themselves up as her protectors.

As she lay huddled in the cart she listened to the noise of increasing drunkenness building up all round her and remembered her original feeling of outrage when she realized that women were banned from marching with the army. It had not taken long before she discovered that they went anyway – but not to fight. Women had been attaching themselves to the column ever since it marched away from Ellem Kirk.

Even from her hiding place, she heard high-pitched shrieks and angry female shouting, like the spitting and cursing of angry cats. Camped behind the food wagons were the tattered tents of a raggle-taggle of women, camp followers who sold themselves for sex for small sums of money. If a man couldn't pay, they'd take his plaid or a pair of boots instead and already many of them were swaddled round with several High-landers' plaids or trudging along in boots too large for their feet. Boots were valuable and could always be exchanged for money later on.

The presence of those women made it all the more essential for Lucy to keep up her boy disguise and it worried her that she might be found out, that her voice might give her away, so she spoke as little as possible and only in a low hoarse voice. Tired out and aching in every bone, with her sprained ankle throbbing, she eventually fell asleep with two questions running through her mind: 'Will I ever find my brothers?' and 'Have I done something terribly stupid by joining up with this army?'

Fourteen

It was still raining next morning, 23rd August, when King James held a council in Twizel Castle. The jubilation that filled him when he crossed the Coldstream ford abated a little when he realized that he was at a turning point. Either he went on, or he took his booty and withdrew.

He'd done that on his first warlike expedition into England, in 1497, when he rode in with a smaller army and caused havoc. It was because of that expedition that Henry Tudor proposed the marriage with his daughter and the Treaty of Perpetual Peace, so James had really scored a victory, which he was now endangering.

But it was so tempting to keep on going this time. When he arrived at Twizel, he found that the English garrison had almost all run away. Those who stayed capitulated as soon as he appeared at the gates, and that put him in a triumphant mood.

'Home,' he said to his major ally in the Borders and the provider of a large part of his foot soldiers, about fifteen thousand men, 'Home, we're going on. We'll split our army in two now. I'll take one half with all the cannon and march on Norham. You double back along the Tweed and capture Wark Castle. When they're both destroyed, we'll both go south to Ford and Etal. I want to wreak vengeance on the English.'

Lord Home, the whey-faced man whose vague appearance gave no clue to his sharp mind and fighting ability, looked suddenly sharp and said, 'It won't take long for me to reduce Wark to a pile of stones. It's half ruined already, but it can't be left as a rallying place for our enemies.'

Robert Borthwick, the master of cannonry, who was in conference with them, spoke up. 'We'll take Norham too, though it's a stronger place. My cannons will reduce it to dust. I'll send them off now.'

James stood up, rubbing his hands. 'And I'm coming with you. I want to see those cannons giving voice in England.'

As Home was turning to leave the castle hall, he paused and said over his shoulder to the King, 'I have a diversion for you among my entourage, my lord. Come to the gate and you'll see it.'

'A diversion?' queried James, laughing. 'This is not the time to present me with a woman, surely?'

'Not yet. This is more in the way of a useful deception. Come out and see.'

They walked together to the huge wooden

gate that now stood ajar to welcome the Scottish army, and Home pulled at the King's arm as they went through. 'Look, what do you see in my bodyguard?' he asked, pointing at a group of men sitting on horses and waiting for him.

James stared at one face after another. Then he laughed. 'By God, you've found me a double. Even I can see the likeness. All he lacks is my beard.'

Home's eyes were narrow and calculating. 'He's growing one. He'll be useful. I'll make sure he's noticed wherever I go and the enemy's spies will never be sure where you are – at Wark or Norham? Here or there? In one part of the battle or in another?'

'Louis of France uses doubles a great deal. He sends them out to play him whenever there's any hint of danger from secret enemies. So do several Italian nobles – they are very afraid of some friend stabbing them in the back. It doesn't protect them from poisoning, though,' said James.

'If he takes a knife in the ribs, he'll be no great loss. He's a horse thief from the Leader valley,' laughed Home and the King laughed with him before raising his hand and saluting Sam Lee, who boldly saluted him back.

Home was right. Wark Castle was half ruined already and fell easily to his forces with little loss of life on either side. The Borderers who

east, and found a redoubt where cannon could be lined up and aimed at the castle's rear.

The danger point of Norham's walls would have been difficult to pinpoint from outside, because it had been superficially repaired to make it look as strong as the rest of the fortifications, but in fact it was only one boulder thick, not ten, for a stretch of about twelve yards – the only weakness in at least a thousand yards of walls.

Before dawn Borthwick's men hauled five cannons up to the crucial spot, and as soon as light streaked the sky they burst forth with plumes of smoke and fire. This time the balls went straight through the stonework and the surrounding walls came tumbling down. Men waiting outside the castle's curtain walls gave howls and yells of delight, and as soon as the dust subsided, rushed forward into the breach brandishing their broadswords. Others who had been waiting in Norham village rushed up to storm the main gate while the guards were in confusion.

By the time the sun was fully risen, the once impregnable castle had fallen and most of its garrison were dead.

When the main portcullis was raised King James rode proudly in and congratulated his soldiers in Scots and in Gaelic. They cheered him so loudly that people huddling in their houses half a mile away heard them.

That night, when James was eating with his closest companions in the semi-ruined main hall, the informer came slinking in and stood at the servitors' doorway from the kitchen.

By the time James was well in his cups the man went up to the table to claim his reward.

'Majesty,' he said bending down so that his head nearly touched the floor.

The King stared down at him and asked, 'What do you want?'

'I've come for my reward, sire. The ring you promised me for showing you where to strike.'

James idly turned the sapphire on his finger and said, 'Ah yes, the ring. Did I say which one I would give you for your treachery?'

Treachery. The word hung in the air and everyone at the table was listening.

'I made your victory possible. You promised to reward me with a ring,' said the man.

'And so I will. Come with me.' James stood up, gathered his silken cloak around him and gestured to the petitioner, who, with a confused look on his face, followed to the main door where two guards armed with axes were standing.

James stopped beside the tallest of them.

'Take him out,' he said, pointing at the man behind him. 'Take him out to a tall tree and hang him!'

The informer dropped to his knees and tried to clasp James round the legs.

'You promised me a ring for my information,' he screamed.

'And a ring is what I will give you. A ring of rope around your scrawny neck. I do not like traitors, of any country.'

The informer's screams could be heard trailing off into the distance while the King walked back to the dining table and sat down. There was a strange ringing in his ears and he felt an elation that he could not explain and did not want to acknowledge even to himself. The eyes of every man in the huge hall were on him while, as nonchalantly as he could he lifted his goblet and drank from it.

He had barely put it back on the table when one of the guards appeared and called out, 'It's done, sire.'

A strange noise like a hiss or a whisper swept through the crowd but all James did was smile and say, 'I don't like traitors.'

When he rose next morning with his head full of alcohol fumes from the night before, he knew he had made a bad mistake.

'What possessed me?' he groaned and wished that he could talk to old Elphinstone about the confusion that clouded his judgement when he ordered the Englishman to be hanged. But the reliance he once placed on his old mentor was gone and he knew that the bishop would no longer treat him with the ease and sympathy he had in the past.

'I need to be shriven,' he said aloud but there was not a priest in his close entourage that he could trust with his confessions, not even his own son Alexander, who, though he was an archbishop, a prince of the church, was not a proper priest, too much his father's son, too tainted with the same faults.

An ascetic-looking Dominican who had marched with a group of Highlanders from Argyll was summoned, but he proved to be too over-awed by being asked to give absolution to a king that James kept his deepest concerns to himself and ended up dissatisfied.

When he went out to show himself to the army, he avoided going near the tree from which the Englishman's body still swung. It was Douglas who mentioned it first, hinting that it would not prove easy to find collaborators on the English side again.

'Will I order my men to cut him down?' he asked, gesturing towards the tree.

James shook his head and brushed him off by saying, 'Leave him up there to show I do not like traitors. I don't deal with them, only with honest and loyal men. Let him hang there to remind all the army of that.'

The other great lords who were gathered around him made murmuring sounds that could have signified agreement or approval but many of them shared Douglas's doubts – as James secretly did himself.

Fifteen

The word of how the King repaid a giver of information spread through the army like wildfire. Some people disapproved but most accepted that James would not deign to benefit from treachery. A traitor to his own country was no better than an unreliable dog, especially when he betrayed in the expectation of gain.

Lucy listened to Willie and Tom talking about the way the King repaid the man who gave him access to Norham.

'The King did the right thing. Hanging's the best thing for a traitor,' said Willie but Old Tom shook his head.

'James is a king. Kings should show mercy. The man gave him Norham Castle and if he didn't want to reward him for that, he should have spared his life. I fear the King's like his father, cruel at heart.'

Could a man who looked so magnificent have a fatal flaw? the girl wondered. Then she remembered how well Sam Lee looked when dressed as the King and she knew he was rotten through and through. Ishbel had been the only member of the Purvis family who did not see that.

Abbess Hoppringle heard what had happened before noon, because she, of course, had scouts in the Scottish army, and she pursed her lips in disapproval. 'The King prides himself on being a knight of chivalry, but that was not a chivalric thing to do. The bad streak in the Stewarts seems to be coming out in James, as it comes out in all of them eventually, I'm afraid. Poor man, I had high hopes for him, because he has a better mind than any of the others and I'm sure he is suffering now...' she said.

The death of the traitor had been pushed to the back of James' mind, however, because the Scottish army was preparing to march again, but already it was shrinking. More of the Edinburgh contingent felt it unwise to travel any farther out of contact with their city and quietly slipped away, consoling themselves with the thought that if the war went against James, they'd be more useful defending their homes than battling in Northumbria. They'd been following him for a month anyway and their obligation was only for forty days. The journey home would take up the other ten days.

Some others, among them Gideon, another of the Lees, had gathered enough plunder in the form of arms and horses from Norham and felt it was time to head for home as well. He said to his brother, 'You stay on. There'll be more pickings to be had when the big battle comes. Don't bother fighting, wait behind and go for jewellery and good daggers on the bodies.'

They shook hands and both instinctively looked over their shoulder where the outlines of the Eildon Hills could be vaguely seen rising through a pale mist, for the rain was still drizzling down. 'Keep an eye open for Sam,' advised Gideon, 'because he's not one to run away when the going's good and I'm sure we'd have seen him by now if he wasn't up to something that he doesn't want to share.'

James allowed his army only a day to recover from their debauches in Norham's stores and cellars, and on the second morning they were on the march again, line after line of men, some on foot and others on horses; toiling lines of wagons bearing cannons; the food stores trundling along in carts with huge wooden wheels.

Because they were heading into enemy

territory and did not know how long it would take to get back, the men who organized the food supply were always on the lookout for additions to their stock and it was Lucy's job to steal hens, ducks, geese or sheep if any were in sight when they passed through farmyards, as they frequently did. As she ran into a yard and scooped up a wandering hen, she was frequently assaulted by a furious farmer's wife who pummelled her back with clenched fists and shouted curses at her. She sympathized with the angry women because she knew how fond her own mother was of the hens that wandered round their mill courtyard.

How were they all at home, she wondered. And most of all, where were Thomas and Peter? Somewhere amid the thousands of men marching around her, she was sure, but trying to find them was like looking for needles in haystacks.

If she had known it, they were again not far away, for they had been roped in to help haul Borthwick's guns. Thomas in particular was brawny and did not seem to mind doing oxen's work. Peter hated it but he could not leave his brother so he stayed too.

An army on the march with no fixed destination in mind was a disturbing place to be. Rumours ran around that they were headed for Berwick or even Newcastle, but the safest bet was that James was going to lay siege to the twin castles of Etal and Ford that lay staring back across the Border, strongholds of disaffected brigands and thieves since time began.

Sixteen

On 30th August, the Earl of Surrey landed in Newcastle with a contingent of English troops. He was an old man, racked by the pain from bones he had broken through a lifetime of campaigning, but his age had done nothing to dull his mind or his determination. King Henry had left him in charge of the defence of the kingdom and defend it he would even if he died in the attempt.

Ever since the Scots crossed the Tweed at Coldstream, the rain had not stopped falling and Surrey's ship made heavy weather trying to get into port. His son, Thomas Howard, the Lord High Admiral, was following his father with more soldiers but the storms detained him, and Surrey was worried about his safety. Another of his sons had died earlier in the year and he was afraid of losing the one that was dearest to him.

On the day he heard the news that Norham

had fallen, Surrey sat in the council chamber of the stark keep at Newcastle and received pledges of loyalty and support from the most important noblemen of the north – Lord Dacre, Sir William Boulmer and Sir Marmaduke Constable – but they told him that amongst them they could raise little more than three thousand men and James Stewart's army was reckoned to be around fifty thousand. Surrey's spies had already heard rumours that the Scots had a hundred thousand men on the field, but that was reckoned to be a wild exaggeration.

Grimly, Surrey looked from face to face and said, 'Fifty thousand is bad enough. We are badly outnumbered, I fear.'

The others agreed but Dacre produced a glimmer of hope. 'Today I heard that Sir Edward Stanley is bringing nearly nine thousand men up from Lancashire. They should be in Alnwick within two days.'

'And the men from Durham and Cumbria are still to arrive,' added Constable.

'But they're only a raggle-taggle, not proper fighting men. Trained soldiers are what we need. At the best we'll be able to raise twenty-four thousand men, and the Scots have twice that,' Surrey told them.

'Queen Catherine is raising another army to come and help us but it has only got as far as Birmingham, and everything will be over by the time it gets here,' said Boulmer, who was of a pessimistic nature.

'We can't wait for it. Numbers are not always an advantage. Tactics matter too. I know James Stewart. He is a man of rash impulse and that should be taken into account when we fight him,' said Surrey.

When young Margaret Tudor was escorted north to meet her husband ten years before, Surrey had been in charge of her entourage and he stayed in Scotland till the marriage was solemnized. During that stay, he had plenty of time to observe James IV and what he saw then had not impressed him.

He could see that the Scots king was courtly, clever and learned but he was also given to acting before he thought. Shrewd old Surrey was determined to keep that trait in mind when planning his strategy.

Constable agreed with him that an early engagement was to be preferred. 'The Scot will want to fight soon because his huge army has almost stripped north Northumberland bare of anything that's edible. They're already running short of food. We should fight while we still have plenty of supplies, because when they run out, there'll be nothing left for any of us.'

Surrey nodded. 'And if this bad weather keeps up it'll be difficult for our ships to bring in more provisions. We're having to pay our soldiers too because they are professionals – the Scots are levies, forced to fight, and will not be draining his treasury. From our point of view, speed is essential. James is marching into England and he'll have to be forced to fight. We don't want him to retreat back across the Border with a lot of booty before we engage with him. He did that sixteen years ago and left devastation behind. This time he has to be stopped for good and all.'

Dacre agreed. The depredations of Scottish raiders were a perpetual thorn in his flesh. 'I think he'll be keen to meet us while he still has a big army. My spies tell me many of them are slipping away already because their forty days of service will soon be up. And there's something else that'll make him eager to meet us. Plague has broken out among some of their men. It's been carried down from Edinburgh, apparently.' This last bit of news caused furrowed brows, because if plague hit one army, it could infect the opposing one too.

Waiting was a fretful time for all of them, but on 3rd September, Surrey's son Thomas Howard, the Lord High Admiral, arrived with a large contingent of troops. He and his father were closeted in discussion for a long time till the old man came out and told his waiting knights, 'That's agreed. It's important to hurry things along. I'll send the Rouge Croix herald to James Stewart with a challenge to meet us in battle on Milfield plain on the ninth of this month. Our men may not be as numerous as the Scots but they are highly trained and disciplined so we should have victory if we fight on level ground.'

'Milfield is a good choice, if he falls for it,' said Dacre. 'It'll draw them down the country and farther away from their supply lines.'

'Let us hope he accepts the challenge,' said Surrey.

As Howard was helping his father to his feet and assist him up to bed, a sweating, muddy messenger was escorted into the keep and a letter he carried taken to Surrey, who looked at the seal curiously and raised his eyebrows.

'From Lady Heron, of all people,' he said to his council.

The letter was a frantic scrawl and he read it out to the waiting men.

' "Help me. James of Scotland has taken Norham and is marching on Ford Castle. Please ask him to spare us. Tell him he need not bother taking a castle with only a woman in charge of it. If you do I will make sure that my brother-in-law joins you and helps your army. His local knowledge, our contacts and the men we have at our disposal could well sway this incursion for you." '

'Huh, it's taken the Herons some time to

pledge loyalty. You can't trust them. They'll be dealing with both sides as usual,' scoffed Dacre, who had many grievances against the family from Ford.

Surrey was a chivalrous man, however. 'But she's alone in that castle. We ought to try to save her from the Scots rabble.'

'If you ask me, my pity will be for them if they try to take her by force,' said Constable, who had the same feelings about the Herons as Dacre.

Howard was more reasoned. 'It would help us to enlist the services of the Bastard Heron. I've heard about him and he certainly knows the lie of the land better than anybody. When he goes on the run neither the Scots nor our men can catch him.'

'Send a letter back and tell the lady that I will intercede with James of Scotland on her behalf,' said Surrey.

'I hope that will be enough to bring the Bastard out of the hills, because I have a few bones to pick with him,' said Dacre.

At the same time another letter was dictated and sent to the Scottish camp outside Etal asking James to bypass Ford because it was garrisoned by a woman. It would be better, Surrey's letter said, to go on to Milfield and have their battle there so they could decide the matter in fair fight.

Seventeen

Ford Castle was a large collection of buildings inside a circling wall that had flat-topped towers at each corner and a long facade staring defiantly back at Scotland. It straddled the side of a range of hills overlooking the River Till, two miles from another Border stronghold, Etal Castle, which was smaller and less imposing but still a formidable base for fighting men.

Together they made a massive obstacle for any invader, but they never cooperated and merged forces because the families that owned each were at loggerheads. Ford had been owned by the marauding Herons for over two hundred years and during that time they had thieved and killed on both side of the Borders, paying homage to no king or overlord. Murder was their way of resolving disputes with their neighbours.

Etal was owned by the Manners family and for two generations an unresolved blood dispute had raged between them and the Herons. A bloody come-and-go miniature war was waged between them until, in the end, the Herons prevailed and forced the Manners to quit Etal and move out though they never yielded it to their enemy. They maintained a small garrison in their castle but it was only there to show face, for the building was poorly kept up and ill defended.

The Scots army was well aware of the local situation, so it was at Etal that James' first attack was aimed after he left Norham.

When he arrived outside it, he laughed when he saw the crumbling state of the walls and said to Douglas, 'We'll take this in an afternoon.'

In fact it only took a couple of hours to overwhelm the men inside the castle and set it alight.

The King did not even bother to ride inside its curtain walls, only turned in his saddle and yelled, 'Now for Ford!' while his army cheered him to the skies.

If he hoped for another easy capture, he realized as soon as he rode near enough to see Ford clearly that he was in for a disappointment. This was an entirely different proposition.

Covering the area of a small town, but entirely surrounded by formidable walls, it was hard to estimate how many men would be waiting inside for the inevitable attack. Neither James nor any of the hardened warriors in his army had ever faced such an apparently impregnable challenge. Norham had been bad enough. This was worse.

From the Till valley floor, James stared up at it and it stared back, stony-faced. Evening was drawing in so he ordered his tent to be pitched and sat down to discuss tactics with his commanders. Leaning his head on his fist, he said to Home, 'Tell me about this castle. Tell me about the man who owns it.'

Home knew the Herons well, for they were a perpetual thorn in his family's flesh, crossing the Border time and time again to seize whatever they could lay their hands on and leaving devastation in their wake.

'It is owned by Lord Heron, but you don't need to worry about him. We have him prisoner in Fast Castle on the coast north of St Abb's Head. It's well named because it is impossible to capture. He'll never get out.'

'How did you get him in?'

'He stabbed the Scottish Warden of the Marches and we went after him.'

'Why didn't you stab him too and put him out of the way?'

'He has an even more formidable half-brother who would lay my land waste if I did that. You may have heard of him. They call him the Bastard and he is an outlaw, hiding out in the Cheviot Hills. Nobody can lay a hand on him.'

James nodded. He'd heard of the Bastard, whose misdeeds were talked of all over Scotland. 'And I suspect you thought you'd keep Heron at Fast Castle till the Bastard paid a ransom for his brother.'

Home shrugged. That was the way things were organized among the potentates of the borderland. 'He hasn't paid up yet,' he said, 'so Heron's still there.'

'And the Bastard is in the Cheviots. Do the Herons have any allegiance to Henry Tudor?'

'They have no allegiance to anybody but themselves.'

'So who is in charge of the castle while the brothers are away?'

'Lord Heron's wife, and she is as fearsome as her husband and her brother-in-law.'

The King was interested. 'I've heard of Elizabeth Heron. Isn't she a great beauty?'

'So some men say, but she's also a she devil.'

Home knew Lady Heron because he had many dealings with her over the years about the misdeeds of her husband and her brother-in-law. When he tried to negotiate over a ransom for Lord Heron with her she had subjected him to a torrent of abuse that reduced him to a trembling wreck.

'She is worse than a man in petticoats,' he told James, who was clearly greatly intrigued.

'And ill-visaged?' asked James.

'Far from it. As beautiful as Morgan le Fay

and as wicked. When she likes she has a tongue that can spin a web of enchantment no matter how hard a man tries to resist it. When she doesn't like she can swear worse than a Belgian mercenary.'

'The men of the Heron family all marry formidable women, women who are their equals. They don't bother to ally themselves with heiresses to bring them lands or possessions. They have plenty of their own anyway and what they want they steal,' Home told him.

'Where did this amazing woman come from?' asked the King.

'From nowhere. People say her father was a horse-coper and she caught Heron's eye at Appleby Fair. The Bastard wanted to marry her too but she chose the elder son – and the legitimate one.'

'And now she's alone in charge of that castle. Will she treat with us?' James asked, and there was a chorus of dissent. He rose from the table. 'But we must try. Send a herald over to invite her to parlay. I'm looking forward to making the acquaintance of this lady,' he said.

Later, when darkness had engulfed the countryside, the herald's body was dumped at the entrance to the King's tent. There was a dagger through his heart.

Eighteen

Elizabeth Heron inspired admiration in men and distrust in women. She was tall for her sex, over five foot eight inches at a time when few men reached that size. Her startling auburn hair flowed like a river down her back and clustered in ringlets round her face, and she had a frank and open way of speaking that took many people by surprise.

From childhood she was determined never to be underestimated and never to be ordinary. In fact there was no danger of either of those things happening to her.

It was inevitable that she would catch the eye of an important man, and as it turned out, she caught the eyes of two, the Heron brothers, a pair of rich rogues with reputations that spread all along the Border country between England and Scotland.

Bastard Heron, the illegitimate brother, saw her first at Appleby Fair riding astride a prancing skewbald stallion with her skirts tucked up around her long, slim bare legs. Speechless at the sight, he dug his brother in the ribs and pointed. When Lord Heron's eyes followed his brother's finger, his jaw dropped.

'Which of us will have her?' he asked his brother.

'I've a feeling she'll do the choosing,' said the Bastard, seeing the way she thrust her mount through a crowd of men who watched her passage with expressions that varied from astonishment to sheer lechery.

She'd heard of the Herons and made sure she crossed their path again that day. Lord Heron was even cajoled into buying a horse he didn't want from her father so she could speak to him. She went off with the brothers that night to one of their strongholds in a wild part of the Lakeland fells and slept with both of them. In the morning she announced that they need not imagine she was only going to be a mistress. She could only be secured through marriage. Who was going to offer?

Amused by her effrontery, they both did and she kept them dangling for a day before she gave her decision. She'd marry the lord, but, if it suited her, she would sleep with the Bastard too because he had a greater power to satisfy her. It was a bargain after their own hearts so they agreed.

Even after the Bastard married the land-rich daughter of a Cumbrian lord, she kept up that part of her bargain. No one, not even she, was sure which brother fathered her five

151

children, but Lord Heron accepted them all.

For eighteen years till 1513 she swept all before her as Lady Heron and never showed a sign of apprehension about anything till she heard that James IV had crossed the Border and was advancing towards her stronghold.

Fast Castle was impregnable, only approachable by a precipitous narrow path along a cliff overlooking the sea. Even the redoubtable Bastard, who could wiggle out of most tight situations, could see no way of extracting his brother from such a fortress. She could not rely on help from the Bastard either. He was outlawed because though his brother was imprisoned for the killing, he was the one who actually plunged the blade into the warden's heart. Even his own countrymen would kill him on sight because he'd preyed on them so badly during his lawless life and they'd be happy to see him out of the way forever. He was on the run in the Cheviots, hiding among trackless hills that were inhabited only by feral goats.

They managed to stay in touch, sending secret messages late at night, and she was also in communication with her imprisoned husband by bribery and similar clandestine methods. Through her, the Herons' nefarious affairs had gone on undisturbed. Till now. It was pointless sending pleas for help to either of her two men. This problem she must solve on her own.

On the day Norham fell, she heard the boom of cannonry coming from the west, and rushed up to the battlements of the northern tower to stare out towards the Tweed. Plumes of smoke could be seen rising into the air and her heart tightened in her chest when she realized how close she was to disaster. For the first time in her life she panicked.

From the top of her tower, she could see the spread of land beyond Branxton village and on to Coldstream. There were no lines of armed men crisscrossing the landscape yet, but if Norham fell they would soon close in on Ford, the place she loved with a passion that was greater than she felt for anything else – greater than her love for her three daughters and two small sons; greater than any emotion she felt towards her husband or his brother, and she loved them all dearly.

Dressed in green velvet with her red hair blowing across her face, she put one flattened hand on the balustrade that ran along the tower top and it seemed to her as if the stone was alive and breathing beneath her palm. The Scots king must not take it, must not sack it, or burn it down! Even if she had to die to save it, she would not spare herself. It was up to her to save it.

She ran down the twisting staircase of the

tower to her chamber, where she dashed off her letter to the Earl of Surrey, who she'd heard was at Newcastle with his army. Up till now none of the Herons had paid more than lip service to the English King and his minions, but this time she needed help.

Nineteen

Next day, outside Etal, James read Surrey's letter, folded it up and decided to take Ford anyway.

'Old Surrey is too much a gentleman,' he said to his son the archbishop, who was looking magnificent in shining armour and a silken tabard.

'What does his letter say?' asked Alexander.

'He wants me to bypass Ford Castle and march on to fight him at Milfield on Friday the ninth.'

'Why there?'

'Because it's flat land. It's easier to win if you stand on raised ground and let the enemy come at you.'

'But that works both ways...'

'He will be fighting with trained foot soldiers. We are not. We'd be better defending ourselves against them. I'm not going to Milfield but I'll accept the date. We'll fight on September the ninth.'

The lady of Ford was too cautious to rely on the success of Surrey's intercession on her behalf. She had another plan. First, as a sweetener for Surrey, she sent off the bulk of her own fighting men to join the English army and then laid in plentiful supplies of food and wine.

She made sure the wells inside the castle were brimming full and there were plenty of buckets stored beside them to quench any fires that might break out. A line of communication was also set up between Ford and the English army and again she pledged her support to Surrey.

After that she decided she'd done as much as she could and, almost undefended, sat in her great hall with children and dogs around her to wait.

She did not have to wait long. When word came that James had marched into Etal Castle almost unopposed, Elizabeth Heron walked to the portcullis over her massive entrance gate and ordered it to be raised. Bit by bit it went up, creaking and groaning till it was fully open and her castle offered no resistance.

The Herons' eldest child, Judith, was sixteen and almost as ferocious as her mother though not so tawny haired. She stood at the postern gate while Elizabeth supervised the raising of the portcullis and said angrily, 'Are you not afraid that people will say you willingly gave Ford up to the Scots?'

'If I let him in, we will not be stormed. He will not fire those cannons of his at an undefended place. They flattened Norham. He lives by the laws of chivalry and no true knight would attack an open gate with women behind it. I must save our castle,' her mother replied.

'You'll be accused of cowardice,' snapped the daughter.

'Cowardice? Don't be stupid. Nobody who knows me will think that. Once I get him in here, I can manipulate him. Though he's a king, he's only a man.'

'By opening our gates to him, you make yourself a traitor, and you know how he deals with them. He hanged the man who showed him how to get into Norham,' said the girl.

'He won't hang me. When I let him in, he'll be my hostage. He'll be in my power,' said her mother, and stepped up to the drawbridge that crossed the moat.

James, glorious in scarlet trimmed with grey fur, arrived at the head of a column of mounted men in the late afternoon when a curtain of rain was sweeping across the rising land on which the castle stood. Stretching out behind him was a large part of his army and their cannons. The line looked endless.

He drew on his reins in surprise when he saw the open gate of Ford, and turned in his saddle to ask his son Alexander, who was riding beside him, 'Do you think it's a trap?'

'Who can tell? She has the name of being tricky,' was Alexander's reply.

Drawn up behind them was a contingent of well-armed foot soldiers, who drew together like an attacking party and brandished their halberds in anticipation of an order to charge, but the King held up one arm to stop them rushing forward when he saw a sole woman walking over the draw-bridge.

She looked like a character from a fairy tale in a cloak of cloth of gold embroidered down the front with huge red flowers. Her face was very white and her startling hair was plastered to her head by the rain. Almost leisurely she came onwards with her eyes fixed on him and when she was within a few feet of him, she held out her hand to the King of Scotland.

'Welcome to the hospitality of Ford, Your Majesty,' she said.

Twenty

After the King received the official challenge to battle from the Earl of Surrey, Lord Wedderburn gathered his five fine sons round him and said, 'We fight the English on the ninth of this month and no matter who triumphs, it will end in slaughter for many people on both sides. We're pledged to fight because we've come this far but I don't want my lands to be without a man to look after them.'

He turned to the one by his side and said, 'You, my eldest son, must go home now before the battle begins and if anything happens to the rest of us, there will at least be one of us left to guard our heritage and look after the youngest boys. If we lose this battle, the borderland will be ravished. Our people will need protecting.'

The other brothers looked towards Alexander with solemn faces because they knew that their father would not give such an order lightly. He stared back, his eyes going from the faces of his brothers to his father, who nodded solemnly and said, 'There is no

fight like my other sons.'

'Give me your blessing, mother,' he pleaded.

'No. I do not bless craven cowards.'

'Not even your first-born child?'

'*No*.' Her face was set and hard. The shadows from the flickering candles made her eyes sink back in their sockets and her nose jutted out like the prow of a ship. She looked like a carved effigy from the top of a tomb. There was no point arguing with her and what she said struck at his heart. He did not want to lose his honour or her regard.

'I will go back to fight,' he said and turned away unblessed.

She watched him go and did not send a word of love after him though her heart was in turmoil. She loved him but she loved honour more. In spite of her double-dealing with both Scots and English for the abbey's sake, she was a Scotswoman at heart and her loyalty was to the King. She could see his faults, but he was her king, God's anointed.

As soon as she heard the abbey gate clang shut behind her son, she went to the chapel and knelt in prayer, asking God to save his life and to forgive her for selfishness in wanting him to survive.

Twenty-One

Wedderburn was not the only man in James' army to have misgivings about the enterprise. Time was running out, the harvest was being gathered in at home; men worried about the security of their wives and children if the English suddenly swung round and marched into Scotland, leaving the Scots army marooned with no one to fight on the wrong side of the Tweed.

The army's numbers were growing less with every day that passed and only men who took their obligations seriously or who had an eye to enriching themselves from plunder stayed. By and large, the Highlanders and the Borderers stayed loyal, keeping together as they marched, encouraging each other with jokes and friendly rivalry.

Now and again the miserable rain slackened and the skies lightened for a short time. When that happened, the outline of the distinctive Eildon Hills could be seen on the western horizon. Eyes were drawn towards them as if they were magnets. The men from the Leader valley knew them well because they had grown up in their shadow. The men from Selkirk, Hawick and Galashiels picked them out too because they knew their homes were within sight of them from another direction. They were like lodestones and symbols of hope, promises that they would see their homes again

Robert Fletcher's face was hard when he stared across the spread of country towards the Eildons one morning. He was finding it hard keeping all his Selkirk contingent loyal. Even some of his brothers were in favour of quietly slipping away.

'We can't. We are bound to stay for forty days and there's still ten to serve.'

'But the food's rotten. The flour's got weevils in it and the ale is sour,' complained one of his brothers.

'You can't run away. It's bad enough that our family name is sullied by Edward refusing to come with us. We must stay and fight till the end. When we go home, we will be heroes.'

'Or dead,' said Dan, the dissident brother, bitterly.

Lucy, perched on a provision wagon, heard the argument and wondered what she would do if she was really a man instead of only pretending. Would she stay and fight? If she was honest the answer was probably 'no'.

When she looked across at the Eildons she thought of the happy days she had spent climbing their slopes, gathering primroses in the spring, or brambles and rosehips in autumn. She wanted to do that again. She didn't want to die.

But she had come so far, it would be almost impossible to turn round and go home now. Her horse was gone – had her uncle reclaimed the grey, she wondered – and she had only a vague idea where she was because by now she was well out of the range of country she knew.

Where were her brothers? She wished she could find them. Not that she was in danger where she was because her two friends who ran the supply trains were kind and protective to her, so kind that she was almost sure that they guessed her secret though they said nothing.

She helped them as much as she could. After the sprain in her ankle healed, she kept forgetting about her pretend limp when she went dashing into farmyards to steal chickens. Old Tom noticed that she was perfectly fleet of foot and raised his eyebrows but only said with a laugh, 'Your leg's better. It must be all the good food we're giving you.'

In fact food was hard to get. The only thing they had in abundance was ale, and when men with empty bellies drank too much of it, trouble was liable to break out. Lucy learned how to hide herself when drunken men were roaming around.

In spite of the hazards, however, she was glad she'd joined the army. From listening to the talk around the cooking fire at night, she learned that both Tom and Willie had been campaigning when they were younger and looked back on those days as the most exciting of their lives.

She wanted excitement too. She wanted to watch cannons roar and castle walls come tumbling down, especially if she was at a safe distance.

More than anything she wanted to be among the crowds cheering the King, who was still her hero though she felt a qualm of disappointment when she remembered how he'd hanged the man who gave him the secret of how to take Norham. Perhaps that was how it was in wars. There was no room for pity or forgiveness.

The days went by in a blur and she had no real idea how long she'd been away from home, but she realized events were drawing to a climax when all the King's followers began to mass on the land between the village of Branxton and Ford Castle, which looked down on them from a distant hillside.

She wandered from group to group in her ragged boy's clothes looking for her brothers, or for anyone she knew, but with no success. Unknown to her, the men from Leader vale were on the far western side of the gathering, encamped among the followers of Lord Home. If she had continued walking a little bit farther she would have found them.

When she turned to go back to her friends and safety, she was almost run down by a group of horsemen led by Home himself. Riding at his side was a glorious figure in glittering chain mail and a silken tabard who was greeted with cheers and wild halloos by the men around her.

'The King! God bless the King,' they called and waved their arms.

Thrown off balance, she crouched on the ground and looked up at the glorious figure – but, she realized in another shock of recognition, it wasn't the King, it was Sam Lee again, looking very confident in his new role and acting the part to perfection, spurring his horse and making it prance. He'd been letting his beard grow, she noticed, and it increased his similarity to James, but in spite of the finery on his back there was something cheap and shifty about him that could not be hidden from people who knew him. His deception would only last for so long.

When Sam rode past the urchin on the ground, he went on to Home's encampment where the Purvis brothers and Sandy Hogg, who had managed to stay together throughout the long trek from home, were sitting with a crowd of pikemen from the Lothians.

One of them was especially kind to Thomas, frequently giving him bits of bannock spread with honeycomb that Thomas loved because he had a very sweet tooth.

'He's like a wee laddie I have at home. He's fond of honey too,' the pikeman told Peter.

'You didn't bring him with you?' Peter asked, and the pikeman shook his head.

'He's not able, he's more simple than your brother, but he's the nicest natured of all my bairns...'

'I'm sorry. My mother and father didn't want to send Thomas but we had to provide two men for our heriot. My father's mill can't run without him and there was no one else to go. I promised to take him back safe.'

The pikeman nodded his head. 'He's lucky to have a good brother. You stay with us when the fighting starts. We can fight off most attackers when we form up in a circle with the pikes sticking out and no one can get near us.'

'I'm not surprised,' said Peter, eyeing the man's eighteen-foot-long weapon lying on the grass. On one end of the long smooth shaft was a sharp point with barbells at the side. Driven into a man it would go right through him.

Thomas, who was sitting beside Peter, was nodding his head sagely though he had no idea what was being talked about. Suddenly he jumped to his feet and pointed into a crowd of men riding by them.

'It's the King! The King!' he cried excitedly. 'Oh, I love to see the King. He's so grand.'

Peter turned in time to see Lord Home go by with a gloriously dressed mounted man at his side.

'Is that the King?' he asked the pikeman.

'Yes, he's wearing his tabard with the golden falcon on it. I thought he was going to Ford Castle, though. He must have come down to join Home. Maybe they'll start the battle soon. I hope they do because I want to get it over and go home.'

Thomas was staring after the King with his eyes ablaze and his hands clasped. 'He's like God,' he said in awe.

The pikeman laughed. 'No, laddie, he's no' that.'

But there were tears in Thomas's eyes when he replied, 'I've never seen anybody so grand. He's my King and I'll kill onybody that tries to hurt him.'

Peter put a comforting arm over his brother's shoulders. 'It's all right, Tom, naebody's going to hurt him. Don't you worry.'

Twenty-Two

Wondering why Sam Lee was still masquerading as the King, and why Lord Home was cooperating in the deception though he must know the real king too well to be taken in, Lucy was wandering through the throng of armed men when she suddenly spotted two other Lee brothers walking along with their swords swinging by their sides and their heads together, planning some misdeed no doubt.

She ran after them and pulled at the youngest brother's sleeve. He stared down at her and it was obvious he had no idea who she was.

'What do you want?' he asked.

'You're one of the Lees, aren't you? I'm looking for the Purvis brothers from Leader Mill. Have you seen them?'

He frowned. 'Do you mean the lad with the brother who's a daftie?'

She hated admitting it but she said, 'Aye, that's them.'

'They're on the other side of the hill, camped beside the men from Hawick and

Selkirk. I saw them yesterday.'

'Are they all right?' she asked.

'What's it to you? They looked fit enough to me. Away you go, you're bothering me with a' your questions.' And he pushed her sharply in the chest, fortunately missing her breasts, which annoyingly had started to swell with such alarming rapidity that she been forced to tie them down with an old scarf she'd found.

In retaliation she snapped at him, 'I saw your brother half an hour ago.'

That stopped them in their progress. Both stared at her. For they'd been wondering where Sam had gone and what sort of ploy he was up to. He was certainly up to something.

'Where is he?' asked the oldest.

'Over there, all dressed up in armour and a tabard with a golden falcon on it.'

The significance of that did not escape them. 'The King's arms?'

'Is it?' she asked innocently and ran away, leaving them to work it out for themselves, knowing full well that if the Lees thought Sam had found a rich source of profit, they'd find him no matter where he was in the camp.

'Your deception's over, Sam,' she thought, exulting.

When she got back to her own safe place by the food carts, she found Tom and Willie

James, and was received coldly although the news he brought was invaluable.

'Your cannon are drawn up in the wrong place. I know where you should move them for an attack on the castle. They should fire at the point where the walls are thinnest on the eastern side. They have never been properly repaired since the last time the castle was besieged, twenty years ago. Your cannonballs should go straight through them...'

'Take Borthwick there and show him,' said James, waving a glittering hand, and it did not escape his notice that the informant's eyes fastened greedily on his huge sapphire ring, the one sent to him by the Queen of France when he was being wooed to attack Henry Tudor in the rear.

'You promised a reward,' said the English traitor.

'I promised a ring,' said James.

'When will I get it?'

'When my army is inside the castle. Go with Borthwick now.'

The two men went off in fitful moonlight, the Englishman in his dark leather jerkin that made him almost invisible, Borthwick in fine clothes and a feathered bonnet. Before they left the encampment, however, Borthwick had the sense to throw a long dark cloak over his shoulders. They walked up the river bank to a point about half a mile to the before he could march on, however.

'Make the shot harder. Send the balls off with more power. These walls must come down,' James shouted in anger at his master of cannonry.

'The walls are at least ten feet thick,' Borthwick snapped back but he kept on bringing up more shot till he was in danger of running out of ammunition. He even resorted to sending men out at dead of night to gather loose balls off the open ground in front of the castle's mound.

'The King is going mad. There must be some way of taking this place,' he complained to his colleagues and one of them said, 'I come from Ladykirk and I know people in Norham. My father used to say there is a back way into the castle. It might be easier to breach there.'

He went off to talk to some local people and when he returned he was smiling. 'I've sent a message into the garrison. I said the King would give one of his golden rings to any man who can show us the best place to breach the defences.'

When darkness fell on the fourth night of the siege, a dark figure slunk along the edge of the castle moat, crossed Ladykirk bridge and sought out the tent with the falcon banner flying from its central pole.

He almost bent double with mock humbleness when he was shown into the presence of went swarming over its walls and running through its labyrinth of corridors in search of something worth stealing were disappointed.

Though he hid his delight from the King, Home was pleased to be ordered to capture Wark because it was rumoured that two ancient war banners that once belonged to the Knights Templars were kept there, and it would be a shaming loss for England if the Scots got hold of them.

He wanted them badly because not only were they valuable, they were symbols of a bygone age, relics from the days of crusading, and he knew that nothing would please the King more than being presented with them. He would be granted any privilege he wanted in exchange.

Sadly, search as his men might, no banners were found and a captured soldier of the garrison told the earl that two men from Berwick had taken them to the town for safe-keeping three days before.

Home was furious. 'So they're in Berwick, are they? If that's true, I'll get them when we sack the town,' he said.

Norham Castle, which was owned by the Bishop of Durham and was much better guarded by a large garrison, proved to be a harder nut to crack than Wark. It stood on the top of a high hill overlooking the Tweed, a solid fortification of red sandstone that looked proud and impregnable. The village of Norham clustered at the foot of the hill enjoying the castle's protection. The flag of Durham's bishop flew from its highest tower. 'Come and get me if you can,' it seemed to say.

For three days James sent wave after wave of men against its massive gates but they never yielded. He sent out parties with battering rams and scaling towers but they too were driven back. His men tried to lob fire over the walls but they were too high. The brass cannons roared and spat out their balls which only seemed to bounce off the castle's stone ramparts.

Wild-eyed with frustration, after three days of trying, the King rode up and down behind the line of Borthwick's long-barrelled cannons, which were drawn up on a ridge of land outside Ladykirk on the opposite bank of the Tweed from the castle. Over and over again they barked out devastating shots but to no avail. Cannonballs, which were thought to be capable of penetrating anything man had ever built, bounced back and rolled along the sward outside the castle walls.

Massed on open ground, facing the river, James' army idled and fretted. Time was draining away. With every hour that passed, he knew, the English army was marching nearer. He had to reduce Norham to ruins argument. Your duty is as much to our lands and people as it is to the King. I order you. Go now.'

'But surely it is my duty as your eldest son to fight alongside you,' he said.

The father shook his head. 'I have four other sons to stand by me. We are contributing enough to Jamie Stewart's foolhardy ambitions. Go now before anyone tries to stop you.'

Reluctantly, because he did not want to be accused of running away, Alexander stood up and buckled his sword round his waist. 'God bless you and keep you safe, father,' he said and then went round each of his brothers to hold their hands as if in final farewell.

'I will take care of our property and all the people on it. I will make sure that no ill befalls your wives or children,' he promised them and they knew he would fulfil that promise.

He rode off towards Coldstream in the dark with his head bent and his shoulders shrouded in a dark cloak. It was almost midnight when he reached the ford. The river was running high because unrelenting rain had been falling since he made his first crossing, but James' ordnance men had been continually working on the river bed, laying bales of straw and pallets of wood to keep a crossing place, and he reached the other bank safely though the water came halfway up his horse's belly in the middle of the flow.

A light was glimmering in the abbey gatehouse and he rode up the short slope of grass to hammer on the closed gate with the hilt of his sword. A grumbling old watchman came to the gate and slid open the little viewing window. 'What do you want at this time of night?' he asked.

'I want to see the abbess.'

'Are you mad? The clock's struck twelve. She'll be asleep. I'm not going to wake her, because she has a sharp tongue that woman. Go away.'

'She will want to see me. She is my mother. Go and waken her.'

He sounded so like her when he spoke that the watchman did as he was told.

It turned out that the abbess was not in bed but sitting at her desk writing a letter to Queen Catherine, wife of Henry VIII, asking her to intercede with the English army not to sack Coldstream Abbey if they prevailed in the forthcoming battle. Catherine and Isabella were on good terms and corresponded frequently. The devout queen had even granted the abbey some lands on the English side of the river because of her admiration for its abbess.

She looked up when the gatekeeper knocked at her door and called out, 'Enter.' Seeing who it was, she frowned and asked, 'What is it? Are you bringing urgent news?' Her abbey received frequent secret messages from both England and Scotland.

'No, madam. I've come to tell you that your son is at the gate asking to speak with you.'

'My son? Don't be stupid.'

'He says he's your son and he looks like you,' protested the gateman.

'Send him up, you fool,' she said. It did not really matter which son it was for she loved them all in her way, but her heart leapt when she thought it might be her favourite. Tears that she could not control sprang to her eyes when she saw tall, beautiful Alexander standing on her threshold.

'Dearest,' she said, holding out her arms to him in a rush of maternal feeling that surprised even her because she thought she had banished all such emotions from her life.

He walked across to her and knelt at her feet, burying his face in her lap. She stroked his head with both hands and for a moment crooned as she used to do when he was a baby. 'What troubles you? Why are you here?' she asked.

He sat silent for what seemed like a long time and then he said in a muffled voice. 'My father has sent me home.'

She drew her hands back as if touching him had burned them. 'Sent you home? Are you ill? Have you been wounded?'

'No. I am fit and well. He says that I must go home so that there will be at least one adult male left to look after our family and our lands if he and my brothers are killed. He says it is my duty. He seems to have some sort of premonition...'

She stood up, making him sit back on his heels and stare up at her. 'Are you really going home?' she asked.

'Yes, I came here tonight to tell you and to ask your blessing.'

'Your father is a fool.'

Alexander shook his head. 'No, he's not. I admire him.'

'He is a fool. And so are you if you do what he asks.'

'But he is my father and my overlord. He has given the care and protection of his property and heritage into my hands. I must do as he says.'

Her voice was cold as ice when she said, 'I come from a family of fighting men who have never turned their back on a battle, never run away.'

'But you have another four sons and a husband in the battle, is that not enough?'

'No, it is not. You are my eldest son. I do not want to see you dishonoured for leaving a battlefield before your sword is drawn. You took an oath to serve your king and you cannot break it. I forbid you to follow your father's base orders. You must go back and home because people will start wanting their corn ground next week ... Oh, I wish I could go!'

They all laughed. 'Lassies dinna fight,' said the man beside her.

She frowned. 'This one could.'

'I dinna doubt it,' said the oldest man at the table, 'but we've only got to supply two men and Jamie and Robert are going for us. Sandy's going for the old couple up the road. Their son died of the fever last winter and they've nobody else.'

She nodded and her eyes went from face to face. Jamie and Robert looked grim but Sandy, the thatch-haired fellow, like her seemed to relish the prospect of battle. He was almost seventeen, the same age as herself, and they'd known each other all their lives, swum in the Leader River in summertime, killed rats and netted rabbits during the harvest, learned to ride the plough horses, teased, pleased and annoyed each other in turn. 'Take me with you, Sandy,' she said, only half in jest, but he shook his head.

Later in the evening, he walked with her down the lane towards her own home and she harangued him, 'I can do anything you can do. I'm a better swimmer than you and better with a bow and arrow. Why can't I go to join the King?'

He sighed. 'Because you're a lassie. It's as simple as that.'

★ ★ ★

At noon seven days later a huge crowd of
people gathered at the junction of four tracks
down hill from the mill. Mounted men came
along the north bank of the Tweed from
Gattonside; others crossed the ford from the
south. Both of the abbeys sent food and baggage trains and a horde of ferocious-looking
warriors rode down from Lauder and Soutra
Hill. Comparing arms and horses, catching
up on family news, men who met rarely
milled around companionably, almost forgetting the purpose of the gathering, till one
of the group from Melrose gave a blast on a
trumpet and shouted, 'Let's get on the way.
We're to muster at Ellem Kirk and it'll take
most of the day to get there. The King and
his army will be in England before us if we
don't start soon.'

They cheered, leapt into their saddles, and
a few more impetuous souls cantered off
towards the east but soon had to slow down
to let the others and the baggage carts catch
up with them. Some of the stragglers held
back for a few moments to turn their heads
and stare at the soft green slopes of the
Eildon Hills that rose as a backdrop behind
them. Hungrily they drank in the smooth
sweep of the triple hills where the gorse still
flowered yellow and a flush of purple was
beginning to mark the stretches of heather.
Every man who looked back at the mystic

hills wondered if he would ever see them again.

The sisters from the mill stood with their parents and watched the men ride away. The miller's wife wept, wiping her eyes on the edge of her apron, and her husband squeezed her shoulder gently. 'Dinna worry, lass, Thomas'll be fine on that bonny horse Ishbel borrowed from the Lees for him. They've got plenty of food and meal in their panniers and Peter'll look after him. I told him to keep out of hand-to-hand fighting, and not to try to be a hero,' he said.

Listening, Lucy thought, 'I'd want to be a hero. I'd want to fight right beside the King. Maybe I could even save his life!' Her mind soared off into daydreams and she was so abstracted that she almost forgot to wave goodbye to the people from Sorley's farm. Ishbel waved to no one either but she never took her eyes off Sam, who looked more handsome than ever in a steel helmet and long leather jerkin. Instead of lusting after him now she hated him and resented the fact that she was carrying his child in her womb.

After the men rode away, the girls spent the rest of the day helping their father at the mill, heaving heavy sacks of meal down from the grinding floor to the store and taking money from the people who came to collect them. Wiping her brow with her sleeve as evening drew in, Lucy reflected how unfair it was that women were not forbidden from doing a man's work, but could not jaunt off to war.

The grey horse was standing at the field gate with its head hanging over, nickering for titbits. She went over to rub the space between its eyes and fished in her pocket for the crust of bread she always kept for it.

'You and I could get to Duns, couldn't we?' she asked the horse, which seemed to nod its head in agreement.

'Then we will! We'll go tomorrow.'

Though she rose at dawn, her parents were up before her. The mill was already grinding when she sat down at the kitchen table and told her mother, 'I think I'll take the grey horse and ride to Aunt Mary's at Duns. I want to hear all the news about the war and she'll know more than we do here.'

Her mother turned back from the range with a look of astonishment on her face. 'It's a day's ride on that old horse,' she said.

'I know. I know the way as well, because I've been there often enough. I'll go straight to Aunt Mary's. Is there anything you want to send to her?'

Her mother's sister Mary was married to a prosperous flesher living on the main street of Duns. She had no children of her own and was always delighted to see her nieces or nephews.

discussing the King with some other men. 'What I can't understand is why he's wasting so much time. Surrey and his men are at Wooler down the hill a bit on their way to Milfield. He should attack them now before any more Englishmen arrive to join their army. But he's vanished.'

'He's not been seen for days,' said one gloomy man. 'We're running out of food and ale and if we don't die of hunger, the plague'll get us all before he makes a move.'

A young man who was standing listening with one arm draped along the cart wheel spoke up. 'He's not vanished. I've just seen him riding through the camp down there with Home. That lad there saw him too. I watched when he almost ran him down,' he said, pointing at Lucy.

They all looked at her and Tom asked, 'Did you see him?'

What to say? How could she explain that the man masquerading as the King was Sam Lee from Redpath? She had secrets of her own to keep. She nodded. 'Yes, I saw him,' she agreed, feeling complicit in a deception that she did not understand.

Twenty-Three

It was an immeasurable comfort to the old Earl of Surrey to have his son Thomas Howard, the Lord High Admiral, by his side during this terrible trouble that had been forced on him in his old age.

James Stewart was playing some sort of cat-and-mouse game, marching into England at the head of a massive army, sacking castles one after the other, but refusing to face up to Surrey's challenge and fight it out.

Everybody knew it would come to a battle in the end, but Surrey bent his grey head and leant on gnarled hands and prayed. The battle could not come fast enough as far as he was concerned.

He was sitting in a filthy room in a tumbledown house by the side of the road that headed south to Wooler. The place was bare of creature comforts, a smoking fire burned in the hearth, hens pecked in the earthen floor around his feet, a scared-looking old woman kept pouring foul ale into a pewter mug at his elbow. A peer of the realm, especially in his old age, was entitled to better. Damn Henry Tudor for his grand ideas about making war in France and clearing the way for the prancing Stewart to advance into England during his absence. Somebody had to stop him.

Spies came into the house all the time and each one bore worse news than the last. James' army still numbered at least forty thousand even though men were disappearing all the time; Surrey knew he had only about twenty thousand under his own banner.

The good news that came told that the plucky little queen Catherine of Aragon, a fiery Spaniard with more guts than ten men, was at the head of her army in Birmingham and marching northwards. But Birmingham was seven days' march away. In spite of the Queen's courage, Surrey knew he could not rely on her help to vanquish the invaders. Time was running out.

The worst news of all, however, was about the English army's supplies. They were dwindling fast, so fast that it was doubtful if the men could be fed for more than four or five days.

Even more worrying was the news that supplies of ale were running out, and armies marched on ale. It was dangerous for men to drink from local streams or rivers because they were often polluted. Surrey had bitter memories of a campaign in which the men had to drink river water and hundreds went down with dysentery. He could not risk that. He must fight, and fight soon.

No reply had been received to his letter challenging James Stewart to a pitched battle at Milfield on 9th September. Today was the 5th, so a reminder had to go out and still he waited for a response which did not come till darkness fell though the distance was not far.

When it arrived, Surrey's son snatched it from the messenger's hand and looked at his father for permission to read it aloud. The old man nodded. 'King James will fight by noon on the 9th but he will take and keep the field at his pleasure, and not at the assigning of an auld and crookit earl...'

Father and son looked at each other, absorbing the insult. Surrey spoke first. 'So he'll fight.'

'He'll fight but he doesn't say where.'

'Where is he now?'

'His army is encamped on Flodden Hill.'

'Presumably he means to fight there.'

'I suppose he does.'

The old man groaned. 'We need local knowledge. None of us knows the lie of the land.'

At that moment a voice rang out from the darkness outside.

'I know the lie of the land. No man knows it better.'

Every man in the room stared at the darkened doorway and the woman who was serving ale gave a scream and threw her apron over her face. A tall, dark outline could be seen in the dim light of their fire.

'And who are you?' asked the Lord High Admiral.

A rough figure with a tangled beard stood on the threshold with both hands raised. The pot-woman started sobbing, 'It's the Bastard. It's the Bastard!'

'She's right. They call me Bastard Heron and if you grant me a pardon for my past crimes, I will come in and join your company,' the stranger said.

If Bastard Heron had been given a first name no one ever remembered it but every man in the room had heard of him, for his crimes were legendary. He had killed and marauded his way round the northern Borders for over twenty years and never been brought to book for his misdemeanours, though many had tried.

'Come in, sire Heron, I guarantee your safety,' said Surrey politely. Like everyone else there he did not know how to address the man who strode into the circle of light in front of the fire and his pale blue eyes stared arrogantly around at the other faces. 'Dacre, Constable, Stanley, Howard, Boulmer, Percy. You're all here, o' course.'

Dacre put a hand on his sword pommel

but Surrey said loudly, 'Leave it be, Dacre. He comes in peace.'

'Peace! He doesn't know the meaning of the word,' said Dacre, letting his hand drop, but his eyes still flashed hate at the Bastard, who walked up to Surrey and bent down to look into the wrinkled old face. 'You are tired, old man,' he said bluntly.

'I am tired, tired near to death,' was the dejected reply.

'You need help.'

'Do I? Who from?'

'I can help you.'

'Can you? How exactly?'

'I can show you how to defeat Jamie Stewart.'

Surrey saw his son curl his lip as if he was going to spit out an angry curse, but again he held up a cautioning hand. 'If I accepted your help, I fear it would come costly.'

'Not too costly. My brother is in prison and I'm tired of running. I'd like us both to be able to sit in our own halls and feast with our family.'

'Or on someone else's,' said Howard, who was not taken in by this.

The Bastard ignored him, only leaned closer to Surrey, who recoiled slightly from the rank unwashed smell that came off him, and said confidently, 'If you agree to my terms, I'll beat Jamie Stewart for you.'

'And what are they?' Surrey felt it was

inevitable that the Bastard would strike a bargain that was advantageous only to himself.

'I want a pardon for my brother and myself.'

Surrey looked over his shoulder at Dacre, who was standing at the back of the room. He had long been the Bastard's enemy and his lands and men had suffered a great deal of death and loss at the Herons' hands. Dacre pulled a disapproving face and shook his head. The Bastard saw this, but only leaned back down beside Surrey and said, 'We need complete pardons – for everything you have against us.'

Dacre could contain himself no longer. 'You're asking too much. There are at least ten capital charges against you and as many against your brother.'

The Bastard turned his head and stared at Dacre. 'That's about right. I've been put to the horn and my brother would be too if the Scots hadn't captured him first. You know what being put to the horn means, of course. It means that any man who meets me on the road can kill me without fear of reprisal.

'I am taking my life in my hands by coming here today to offer you my help. Don't you value that?'

In spite of himself Surrey was impressed by the villain's confident composure and his dignity.

'You are certainly daring. We could kill you now and no one would know. What can you do for me that will justify granting you such an overwhelming pardon? You're not claiming to be a wrongly accused innocent man, are you?'

The Bastard laughed sarcastically. 'No! I am proud of what the Herons have done. We've reduced men like Dacre here to shivering dogs. I am offering you my skill and my knowledge of this countryside. I know every stream, every river crossing, every bog and moss, every track, every place where men can hide. No living man knows this country better than I do, not even my own brother. I know exactly where Jamie Stewart's army is waiting at this moment. I've stood at the gate of his tent. I know how you can beat him.'

Stanley leaned over his father's shoulder and stared into the Bastard's face. 'Why should you do this for us? You are no more a friend of King Henry than you are of King James. These are the debatable lands and you are a very debatable ally that can change like the weather.'

The Bastard straightened up and stared him back. 'And that's another thing I know. I know how to use this country's weather. Look out of that door. The rain is still heavy, isn't it? That could be to your advantage. I'll tell you how to use it. I am willing to help

180

you because I want the pardons, and because I want to save Ford Castle, my family's home, from being burned to the ground by the Scots.'

'Your sister-in-law has already written asking me to intercede with the Scots king about the safety of her property,' Surrey told him.

'Did you do so?'

'I did and he ignored my letter.'

'And now he's moved into Ford. I was there when he came walking into our courtyard. My sister-in-law knows how to cope with him, though, and she will tell me his plans. I'm in constant touch with her.'

'But if he is installed at Ford she must be his prisoner, and with the castle swarming with Scotsmen it's hard to believe you can go in and out as you please,' scoffed the constable.

The Bastard gave a wide grin that transformed his menacing face into one of considerable charm. 'Never underestimate the Herons,' he said, pulling out a stool and confidently sitting himself down on it in front of Surrey, leaning his elbows on the rough table and saying to the weary earl, 'Are you ready to listen to me? Are you prepared to agree to my demands?'

Surrey looked doubtful. 'How can I promise the safety of Ford Castle if Jamie Stewart is in there already?'

The Bastard waved a hand. 'First things first. Elizabeth will guard the castle. Let me give you a bit of advice to begin with. The Scots are encamped on Flodden Hill and if Jamie has any sense they won't be moving off it unless they're tricked into doing so.'

He had their attention now and they clustered round, listening to him. 'How tricked?' asked Stanley.

'He's not going to come down here to Wooler to meet you. He's not going to engage you in battle at Milfield on flat ground. You'll have to leave here because he won't come to get you. He'll sit up on Branxton Heights and wait for you to attack him before you run out of food and ale or for the plague to get you all.'

'He needs food and ale too and the plague has killed a lot of his men as well,' said Howard.

'But his lines of communication are better than yours. He controls the ford at Coldstream, which is within sight of Flodden. His supplies come over all the time. Your supplies have to come from Newcastle and the Scots are already marauding up and down the road. On my way here I passed a long baggage line of carts taking fresh supplies to the Scottish army. They'll be feasting by tomorrow. Will you?'

None of the Englishmen said anything as he looked boldly from face to face, though some of them did not meet his eyes.

'You must push for a battle before your men die of thirst or the running sickness,' he told them.

Surrey sighed. 'What you're telling me is what I already know, but he's in a strong position. A defender on high ground is hard to shift.'

'I know how to shift him and I've stated my price. Do you accept or not? If you don't I can cross over and offer my services to Jamie Stewart.'

'He'll hang you like he hanged the traitor at Norham,' said Dacre angrily.

'No, he won't. I'm too big for a hanging. He only hangs little men.'

'I suppose we'll have to accept your bargain, though a pardon from me won't give you release from your punishment for mortal sins. God will have his revenge on you,' said Surrey sadly.

The Bastard laughed. 'How do you know that God isn't a Heron? I'll deal with him when my time comes. Prating priests don't scare me because I have the Devil on my side. Do you accept? Do we get our pardons?'

Surrey held out his hand. 'You have them, provided we win the battle. Now tell me how to defeat the Scots.'

Twenty-Four

Though she was far away from the scene of war, Margaret soon heard about her husband's successful attack on Norham, and about the reward he handed out to the man who made that victory possible.

The story was relayed to her by Archibald Douglas when she sat in the window embrasure of the rooms she'd moved into at the very top of the huge palace, rooms her people referred to as the Queen's Bower. The more kindly ladies in her entourage said she spent so much time in those high rooms because from them she had an uninterrupted view along the road leading to England.

'She's watching for Jamie's return,' they said, but Margaret had inherited a good share of her father's caution and her motives were more dispassionate. She watched obsessively from her bower, not for the King, but for any sign of approaching bands of fighting men.

If James lost the coming battle, or if he was killed, other great Scottish lords, who were always on the lookout for seizing power, would want to seize her son, and might even want her out of the way because before he rode off to war her husband had left orders that she was to be the heir's guardian.

A quick escape might be necessary, so she kept her watching vigil and had also made arrangements for herself and the baby prince to flee to the River Forth, where a boat was kept waiting to carry her south to her brother's protection.

As a child she was always able to bully Henry and did not think she'd lost her power over him though he was proving intransigent about the jewels from her dowry, but that was because he was so greedy and needed reprimanding, she reckoned. He had always been indulgent towards her so she should find a safe haven with him.

She showed shocked disappointment when Douglas told her about the summary hanging at Norham. She was not an over-sensitive or sentimental woman, but she was a pragmatist and felt her husband had committed a serious error.

'No one on the other side will ever provide him with secret information again,' she said.

'That is what everyone fears. Your husband seems to have lost his sense of caution since he went to war,' said Douglas.

She looked sharply at him, sensing he knew more than he was telling her. Douglas's sources of information were even better than hers.

'Where is my husband at the moment?' she asked and saw his eyes slide away from hers.

'The last I saw of him he'd reduced Etal Castle and was advancing on Ford. He will be there now.'

'When will he fight?'

'Surrey has challenged your husband to meet him at Milfield on the 9th of the month.'

'Will he go?'

'I can't tell.'

She allowed herself to be sidetracked as he asked after the well-being of the little prince. When the child had been shown off they diverted themselves by playing their lutes together. It was a very pleasant meeting and after he left, Margaret realized how much she anticipated his visits.

Life had not been easy for her recently. Her conviction that she had fallen pregnant after meeting the King at Holyrood seemed to be true.

She was nauseous every morning, as she invariably was in early pregnancy, but in spite of that, she brightened up in Douglas's presence. He always showed gentle concern for her well-being, tucking cushions in at the small of her back and mixing her a wine negus into which he put leaves of mint and rosemary, both of which he said were good for women in her condition.

'My mother always drank that negus and she bore five fine sons,' he told her.

Unused to male cosseting, Margaret blossomed in the warmth of his concern and allowed the thought to cross her mind that if Jamie was to die in battle, she would take Douglas as her second and more loving husband. What she did not realize was that he had exactly the same idea and his motives were not romantic but purely dynastic.

At the same time as he told her the King was besieging Ford, he brought news that the plague had burned itself out in Edinburgh. 'It's safe enough to take the baby prince there now,' he said, but Margaret shook her head. Though she gave no reason for her refusal it was because she was unsure of the outcome of her husband's foray into England.

Bishop Elphinstone and she had agreed that James's nature might be his downfall when it came to fighting. 'He's too impetuous,' Elphinstone said and Margaret agreed.

If her brother's army won the battle, the English would probably march on the capital city, where the garrison was much depleted by having sent off so many men to the Scottish army. She did not want to be in Holyrood when Edinburgh fell.

She often thought of the guard Robbie Mackay who had driven away the mysterious messenger of doom in the middle of the summer night. Had he joined her husband's army? Would he lose his life, as the midnight messenger predicted? She wondered where Elphinstone had found the bell-ringing man, because he really seemed to have the power of prophecy. Her superstitious soul was chilled by the memory of him and his terrible litany of deaths to come.

On the day she refused to move to Edinburgh, she received more news of James' acceptance of Surrey's challenge to fight on 9th September, and in the middle of the night, she woke with a start and sat up in bed, with her heart racing and sweat breaking out on her forehead.

What's wrong? Am I going into premature labour again? she wondered, but sank back reassured against her pillows when she realized that she had no pains. This time the disturbance was in her mind and not in her body.

Disquiet filled and immobilized her. She had never felt like this before, but she was in the grip of an absolute certainty that something dreadful was going to happen. She knew that at the very moment she woke in terror her husband was making some terrible mistake. Exactly what that mistake was she did not know; it was only 4th September, so the battle could not have started yet, but something was very wrong. The Queen felt sure a woman was involved in it.

For the rest of the night it was impossible for her to sleep and she lay arguing with herself not to give in to her overwhelming jealousy and resentment at being unloved by James. News of him will come in the morning, she told herself as she lay watching for first light.

As usual the bringer of the information was Douglas. Looking solemn, he turned up in her chamber where she was sitting with her ladies in the grey light of a rainy morning.

'What news from my husband?' she asked in as light a tone as she could manage.

He smiled tightly and told the good news first. 'A messenger tells me he's taken Ford Castle without one cannon being fired.'

She turned on her stool in surprise and dropped her embroidery needle. 'Ford? It's meant to be very strongly defended, isn't it?'

'He's in Ford at the moment,' said Douglas.

'In Ford? Isn't the chatelaine of that place a notorious woman?' Margaret was well aware of her husband's susceptibility to dangerous women.

He shook his head and pretended to misunderstand. 'She cannot do anything to harm him. The Scots army is drawn up at her gates.'

'I'm told Lady Heron, the chatelaine, gave it up willingly to the King. My sources say she walked out and surrendered to him. He is staying in the castle with her.'

Elizabeth, Lady Heron! Margaret felt sick. Gossip about that woman had spread beyond national boundaries, and at that moment the Queen knew she'd been right to feel so strange in the middle of the night. Had she woken when the notorious Lady Heron took James Stewart into her bed?

She remembered the words of the young intruder in the central courtyard of the palace on the last day she saw James ... 'Meddle with no women nor use their counsel, nor let them touch thy body, for if they do, thou will be confounded...' Elphinstone, who instructed the messenger, was always disapproving of James' womanizing, of any womanizing come to that, and was continually preaching of the dangers of giving in to lechery.

She shared his misgivings as far as her husband was concerned and the warning words were burned into her brain. Even on the eve of a battle, James was capable of being distracted by a woman, especially a woman like Lady Heron, who, if only half of the stories about her were true, was a formidable force – and an Englishwoman, of course.

Had he tarried, procrastinated, consorted with the enemy and neglected the business in hand? Had he sealed his fate, and with it, the fate of Scotland? She looked at the faces of the women around her and knew they shared her fears; some tried to hide the malice in their eyes and only a few looked at her with pity.

Twenty-Five

'Welcome to the hospitality of Ford,' said the red-haired woman.

As James walked towards her, he saw that she was tall and shapely, truly as glorious as men said, for he'd heard her compared to Morgan le Fay, as beautiful and as dangerous. Lady Heron was a woman very much to his taste. The blood rushed through his body and he felt his penis stiffen in anticipation of going to bed with her, for he knew that would happen.

He had been without a real sexual challenge for a long time. Because he was the King, no woman refused him, but this one was the enemy and would need persuading one way or another.

Equally confident, Elizabeth Heron watched him walking towards her and could read his mind. As far as she was concerned, there was no doubt that she could seduce him and it would not be too distasteful for he was fine-looking man, like a well-bred stallion. His legs were long and well muscled and he walked with a casual ease that showed he would be adroit in bed.

No, indeed, it would not be too much of a sacrifice to yield to him. Anything she could do to save her beloved Ford was worthwhile.

'Delay Jamie,' the Bastard said on his last late-night visit, 'you can do it better than anyone. Distract him and loosen his tongue. Anything you find out will be useful. I don't care what arts you use and neither will your husband. If Scotland is brought to its knees, Fast Castle will crack open like a walnut shell, and if I insinuate myself with Surrey, my brother will come home and our power will increase in Northumberland. Dacre and his allies won't bother us again.'

When the news came from her scouts that the Scottish king's army was within a mile of her castle, she'd gathered up all the children and shut them in the innermost tower with a few armed men to guard them.

Most of the men of her garrison had gone away to join the Bastard, but the wells, larders and granaries were full and she was gambling on her own powers to overcome the danger.

There was no trembling of her hands as she dressed herself grandly and stood by the closed portcullis gate awaiting the arrival of the enemy.

When a lookout called down from the tallest tower that the Scots were drawing up in formation facing her castle and their cannons were in place, she ordered the drawbridge to be lowered and walked out in all her glory without an escort. It was easy to pick out the King for she had heard tales of his flowing black hair and red beard. Fixing him with her eyes she walked straight towards him...

'Welcome to Ford,' she said and bowed her stately head. Pride would not let her curtsy.

With a touch of his long curving spurs, he urged his horse towards her till he was so close that he could reach down and touch her chin which he gently tilted up so that she was looking full into his eyes. His were hazel but hers were a green that echoed the colour of two fine emeralds that swung from her ears.

She did not flinch from the touch of his fingers on her face, just stared boldly back at him for a few seconds, then shifted her eyes to look over his shoulder at the crowd of knights and courtiers who were following him onto her drawbridge. Glorious in their heraldic colours, with glistening armour covering their chests and steel helmets on their heads, they seemed an invincible horde.

The young man riding nearest to the King sat casually on a huge chestnut horse with a white blaze down the middle of its face. The pennant flying from his lance showed the arms of an archbishop.

'That's his son, the one by Margaret Drummond,' she thought, and the idea came to her that her daughter Judith should be directed to suborn him. He was a handsome young fellow so it could be an experience for the girl, and if she were to fall with child, royal blood would be introduced into the Heron family. Elizabeth took pride in her skill at breeding good horses, knowing which mare to match with which stallion. Why not use her gift with humans too when such a glorious opportunity presented itself?

'Our doors are open and we have prepared food for you,' she told James, who dismounted and in courtly fashion kissed her hand. Then she placed her fingers lightly on the crook of his arm as if they were about to start dancing, and without speaking they walked together through the huge stone gateway into the heart of Ford Castle.

He stopped in the middle of the inner courtyard and stared around appreciatively. The place was huge, bigger than he expected, and he knew that if it had been well defended and he'd been forced to lay siege to it, the task would not have been easy.

Strangely, for such a formidable stronghold, it seemed very empty. Was the dangerous-looking woman by his side playing a trick on him? Was she leading him into an ambush? Were armed warriors waiting in hiding to attack him when his suspicions were allayed? But only a handful of men stood behind Lady Heron at the gateway and none was heavily armed. Some serving women clustered in open doorways or looked cautiously out of upper windows.

'You are very trusting to garrison your castle with so few soldiers,' he said to Lady Heron.

She grimaced. 'Most of them ran away when they heard the Scots were coming. Since Norham, your army is much feared, sire.'

'By you too?' he asked.

'Of course,' she said demurely and dropped her eyes. They walked on into the great hall, where a long table had been laid in anticipation of a feast. James sat at the head of the table and the lords of his close escort followed his example while orders were sent out to the soldiers waiting to attack Ford, telling them to pitch camp and wait for the King's return.

If there were few Heron soldiers to be seen, there were plenty of serving boys, who ran to and fro carrying huge roasts of meat, more succulent than any James' knights had seen for a long time. The boys filled and refilled tankards of mead and ale till heads swam and the noise echoed and re-echoed off the high vaulted roof.

Lady Heron sat beside the King of Scotland and fed him the tastiest bits of meat and fish off the end of a silver knife. Each time he took the titbit into his mouth she lightly licked her own lips in such a way that he wanted to throw away all caution and take her straight to bed.

'She's the enemy. Don't trust her,' said a wary voice inside his head but it was easy to ignore.

Farther down the table his son was seated beside the daughter of the house, who was far less accommodating than her mother. She sat well back from Alexander and frowned when he pledged her health as he downed the contents of his tankard. His face was growing redder and his speech becoming slurred.

'Whatsh your name?' he asked the girl.

'Judith,' she said coldly and clearly.

'Judith? She'sh in the Bible.'

'Is she really.' The tone was flat.

'Are you a widow?' was his next question.

This time she was surprised. 'A widow? I'm not even married yet. I'm only sixteen.'

'My stepmother married when she wash fourteen,' he said.

'Poor thing,' said Judith, 'my mother thinks I should have time to make my own choice. She did.'

'And has your eye been caught yet?'

'No.'

'I'm glad you're not a widow,' he mumbled.

'Why?' she wanted to know.

'Because Judith in the Bible was a widow and she cut off the head of the King's general and right-hand man, Holofernes. Cut – it – right – off,' he said slowly, making a sawing movement across his own throat. She watched his moving hand with fascination. He wore beautiful rings on every finger, even on his thumb.

'It must have hurt,' she said in a coldly joking voice.

'Yes, it must. I'm my father's right-hand man so I'm glad you're not Judith, the widow...' he said again.

'You shouldn't tell me Bible stories. They might give me ideas,' she replied.

After a couple of hours of feasting, when she saw that her enemy's suspicions were swamped by wine, Lady Heron left the table and took her women over to the biggest tower in the castle, where they clustered in one of the large first-floor rooms and looked at her with questioning eyes. They knew she was up to something dangerous when she closed the shutters and lowered the bar on the door so no one could get in.

'You're all safe from those slavering Scotsmen in here. I've given orders that they should be given as much mead as they can swallow. They'll pass out soon.'

Her daughter was staring at her mother with anger clear on her face. 'What do you think you're doing? How could you treat that man as if he is an honoured guest?' she asked.

Lady Heron stared coldly back at the girl. 'I'm saving Ford. I'm saving our lives too. If he'd turned his cannons on us, we would all be dead by now.'

'I'm so ashamed,' said Judith in a trembling voice.

'Save your shame for something more worthy of it. I know what I'm doing. Come into my chamber and let me talk to you,' said her mother.

When they were alone, the mother said, 'Don't be deceived by my smiles. This is a serious business. Your uncle was here two nights ago. He told me to detain Stewart for as long as I can. Surrey needs time to get his army back from Wooler and be ready to fight because it looks as if the Scots are not going to come down off Flodden Hill. There's only one way that I can delay a man like Stewart and I'm going to do it.'

Judith listened bleak-faced. She knew what her mother had in mind.

'Don't look like that,' said her mother, 'you're a Heron. You're not a fool. I'll sleep with him, of course. I'll make him talk about his plans and I'll send them on to Surrey.

But most of all, I'll keep him off the field for as long as possible. You could help.'

'Me? How? I won't sleep with him!'

'Not him. But you could sleep with that son of his and stop him urging his father back to fighting. He may be an archbishop but he has his father's nature. Between us we could entrap both of them and leave their army without leadership for as long as Surrey needs.'

'I can't. I can't!'

'Why not? He's handsome and he'll be virile enough when he sobers up. Don't pretend you're shy. You're not a virgin. I know about that young lad in the stables. Besides, I'd rather a King's son fathers your first child than a stable boy.'

'That was only once or twice,' Judith stammered.

'I don't care if it was every night for a month. You have to start sometime and it might as well be with him. Now put your experience to good use and turn it on St Andrews.'

'But I don't like him.'

'That's not important. Do you imagine I like his father? He's my enemy. My husband, your father, is his prisoner. If I'm ever to see him again, James Stewart must be beaten. And most of all, if Ford Castle is to be left standing, he must be won round. Did you see the cannons he brought with him? I don't want them blazing away at us and bringing down our walls. We're only women. We can't go out jousting or leading charges. We have to use what we are good at. That's why I'll have James Stewart in my bed tonight, and if you are my true daughter you'll have his son in yours.'

That night King James fell into a drunken sleep in the most magnificent chamber of Ford Castle. It was on the first floor of a large square tower that stood at the farthermost west end of the range of fortified buildings. Panelled with smooth and shiny elm, the walls were hung with tapestries that quivered whenever a wind blew from the north. In the middle of the floor was a huge, sumptuous bed hung with heavily embroidered scarlet curtains, piled with pillows and covered with a wolf skin.

In the farthest corner of the room was a small door that led to a curving wooden stair rising to the room above. The door was unlocked.

Early in the morning, before dawn broke, it creaked open and a figure in a long white shift carrying a candle slipped through it, hurried over the floor and pulled open the bed curtain. The naked King lay on his side with his face sunk into a pillow and his thick hair falling over his shoulders. The wolf skin was pulled up between his legs but it stopped short at his waist and the flickering candle flame showed the penitential iron chain encircling his waist.

Curious, Lady Heron touched one of the links with her forefinger, but he did not wake. Laying the candlestick down on a side table, she snuffed it out and slowly slid into the bed. The room was as dark as a coal pit and the man slept on.

She took off her shift and lay on her back, still and silent for a long time, until the first grey light of dawn appeared in the cracks of the shutters that were closed over the window embrasures. Then she turned on her side and first laid a gentle hand on his hair, then slid her other hand over his waist and gently took hold of his flaccid penis. With practised skill in the arts of love, she woke him.

He'd been dreaming about his mother. She appeared often in his dreams, sometimes as wistful as she had been in life and at other times looking happier and more like Margaret Drummond than her real self. Those dreams always made him sad because his mother, Margaret of Denmark, had been a kind and gentle woman who made much of him, stroking his hair and murmuring sweet words in his ear. His loathing of his father was rooted in the knowledge of the way he treated his wife, scorning and shaming her by his preference for a troop of preening catamites.

And, worse than that, he was sure his father had poisoned her. It served him right that two years after her death he was killed himself, and his son looked the other way as the deed was done.

Uneasily dreaming, he turned his face into the pillow so that the hand that was smoothing his head could go on ... then he realized that the other hand was comforting him in a different way.

When he opened his eyes it was half light and he looked into a face which was almost hidden by a falling cataract of glorious hair. Reaching up, he grabbed a handful of it and roughly pulled her face down onto his.

There was no suggestion of love or romance in their encounter for either of them. It was purely animal passion, and both were passionate people. When they finally fell apart, she groaned, 'Why do you wear that horrible thing round your waist? It cuts into my skin.'

He said nothing, only lay and stared at her as if he was seeing her for the first time. This, he realized, was his female equivalent. A woman as sensual and uncaring of emotion as himself. He reached out to pull her on top of him and she fended him off.

'No,' she said.

'A sudden attack of fidelity, my lady?' he asked mockingly.

'No, an attack of skin rash. That chain hurts me. I can't bear it chafing on my skin.'

'I never take it off,' he said grimly.

She slid a hand over to him again, touched a link of the chain and asked coaxingly, 'It must open somehow. If you develop a big belly, what will happen then?'

'A blacksmith will make another link for it. It has been enlarged several times since I first put it on.'

'Like shoeing a horse,' she jeered.

'Exactly.'

'But seriously, I know it must have a secret clasp. Won't you take it off? Our coupling would be even better without it.'

'I vowed to St Ninian never to remove it. I will die with it on me.'

'Won't you take it off for only a short time to please me?'

'*Never.*' He was very definite.

She knew there was no point arguing more and leaned over to kiss him as a gesture of acceptance.

Twenty-Six

Within sight of the room where James lay in bed with his enchantress, his army was gradually massing on Flodden Hill, in the middle of a small range called Branxton Heights, but he did not rise to look out at them.

They came from every direction, lines of men tired of marching, tired of waiting for the final clash which could spell either death or victory. Harried along by mounted grandees, organized, shouted at, ordered here or there, they did as they were told, shouldering their meagre possessions, hiding what was left of their private supplies of food from each other, wondering which lord they should attach themselves to in order to be safe.

Most of the Border men, including the contingents from Lauder, Melrose, Selkirk and Hawick, were formed into groups of infantry issued with pikes and joined in with the men under command of Lord Home, their local overlord, who had a fearsome reputation as a wily fighter.

A few of the other Borderers opted to

follow the old Earl of Douglas, who had an equally admirable reputation for winning battles and who organized his soldiers in the same way as Home. They would fight on foot because they were no longer mounted and their horses were kept with the baggage and food wagons behind the lines. Among Douglas's men were the Purvis brothers and Sandy Hogg. The Lee brothers were there too and they were already secretly marking out which horses they would steal to make their getaways on as soon as the fighting started.

At midday on 6th September, Peter, Thomas and Sandy sat in a huddle beneath a thick-trunked oak tree that spattered them with acorns while heavy rain still fell, and stared out across the vast field of armed men.

'Do you think it will come to a fight soon?' Sandy asked Peter, who was sitting with one arm round the shoulders of his brother.

'I hope so. I'm tired of all this. I want to go home and I promised my mother I'd keep Thomas safe. He's tired now and doesn't understand where he is. I'm worried about him.'

Sandy reached over and put his last small piece of bannock in Thomas' hand. 'You'll be all right, won't you, wee Tom? You'll do what Peter and I tell you when the fighting starts.'

Thomas, whose wet hair was plastered round his face, looked up and gave a crooked smile. 'I want to see the fighting. I want to see the King.'

'A lot of folk want to see the King. I was hearing that he's disappeared. One of the Selkirk men said that there's a rumour he's run away,' said Peter bitterly.

'Run away!' Sandy was genuinely shocked. 'He'd never do that. Anyway, he can't have gone far because I saw him riding through the camp yesterday.'

'I'm glad to hear it. Listen, I'm hungry and they say more food wagons arrived from Kelso this morning. Let's go behind the hill and try to find them.'

They rose, shook themselves and headed for the south, where they knew the supply train would be drawn up. As he stared towards the horizon, Peter saw that the rain clouds had momentarily cleared away from the western horizon and swimming dim into his sight came the outlines of the three Eildon Hills.

His heart ached at the sight of them. I want to go back there, he thought, I want to stand on my birth soil again. I want to take my poor simple-minded brother back to the place where his father, grandfather, great-grandfather and many more before them were born. What madness brought us here to fight and perhaps die for a man who does not even know we exist? He did not say it, however, because he knew that Tom revered the idea of the King and Sandy was almost as loyal.

The rumour about new supplies proved to be correct. A line of carts was drawn up behind a long stone wall and armed men were guarding them. Old men and young boys were standing on top of the carts dividing out provisions to waiting lines of servitors of the various contingents of the army.

Peter spotted one of the pikemen he had spoken to earlier and pulled at the sleeve of his leather jerkin. 'Can you get us something to eat?' he asked.

The man looked over and saw the shivering Thomas. 'Oh, it's you. I'll try.'

When his turn came, he looked up at the urchin who was handing bags of oatmeal and a churn of butter down to him and said, 'Can you spare something extra for a poor simpleton laddie?'

The urchin stood up abruptly and asked, 'A simpleton? Where is he?'

'Over there, by the wall. His brother's with him.'

To his surprise, the urchin leaped off the wagon and ran across the grass to the wall where the forlorn trio were standing. 'Oh, Peter, oh, Thomas, oh, Sandy!' he cried and gathered the simpleton in a close embrace.

Thomas knew her at once. 'I'm awful

hungry, Lucy,' he whimpered.

With tears running down her cheeks she pulled him towards the wagon. 'Come with me. I'll get you food. I'll get you a big fat chicken ... Oh, I've been looking for you everywhere. I was so afraid that you'd been killed at Wark or Norham or someplace else. It's a miracle that I've found you.'

Sandy and Peter followed her with amazed expressions on their faces. 'What are you doing here?' Peter managed to ask at last when he realized that this really was his sister who he thought he'd left safe at home.

'I wanted to see the war. I followed the next day. I took the grey horse but he went lame and I left him in a field at Ellem Kirk. There was plenty of grass for him.' Words were pouring from her but her eyes were also shining with the excitement of finding them.

'How did you get father to allow you to come?' Peter asked.

'He didn't know I was leaving. I went to Aunt Mary in Duns first and then I just rode on behind the army.'

'You're mad, Lucy,' said her brother.

'Don't call me that. Here I'm Hoppy.' She looked over her shoulder to where Old Tom was heaving down sacks of vegetables and apples towards the waiting throng. But he had been listening although he was busy.

'It's Lucy, is it? Willie and I wondered what your real name is,' he shouted down.

She looked up at him. 'So you knew?'

'I guessed you're a lassie from the beginning. Willie and I thought we'd better take care of you and try to get you safely home again when all this is over.'

Tears filled her eyes again when she said, 'Oh, thank you. I never guessed that you knew.'

'That's because you're just a silly lassie,' said Tom tolerantly.

'These two are my brothers and this other one is my friend,' she said, pointing at Thomas, Peter and Sandy.

Tom's face was grim when he looked at them. 'Are you with Home?' he asked.

'We've been put in with Douglas's men,' replied Peter.

'He's as good a soldier as Home. God be with you all when the fighting starts. We'll look after your sister. Come back for her when it's over, if you can,' said the old man.

Hiding a chicken beneath Sandy's jerkin and carrying a bag of oatmeal and a flagon of ale, they headed back to their shelter in the woods. The rain had stopped but streaks of dark purple marked the western sky. Peter looked at the clouds grimly and said, 'It'll rain again tomorrow, I think. We'd better light a fire to cook the chicken and it'll dry out some of our clothes and our boots too.'

They slept that night huddled round the

flames in their shirts while the fire dried their boots and jerkins, feeling much better because they'd eaten well. When they woke next morning and stood up to stretch, Thomas suddenly cried out and pointed out to the field in front of them and called, 'Look. The King's no' run awa'. There he is. That's his flag!'

Before they could stop him, he dashed off, bare feet skidding on wet grass, towards the group of knights around the King who was sitting easily in his saddle, gazing around and receiving the obeisances of foot soldiers around him. Thomas burst through the crowd, calling excitedly, 'Ye didna run awa' did ye?'

When he reached the King's horse's shoulder, he looked up and his face changed. 'Ye're no' James, though, are ye? Ye're Sam Lee.'

Turning round, he pointed over his shoulder at the richly caparisoned man on the horse and yelled to the crowd, 'It's Sam Lee. I ken him. He's a horse thief.'

The man on Sam's right leaned down and swiped with his sword at the shouting lad. At the moment when the blade could have sliced off Thomas's head, his horse shied back and he only succeeded in striking a glancing blow. Then he gave a shout of command and Sam with his escort spurred their horses and galloped away.

Peter and Sandy ran up and pulled Thomas to his feet. Blood was pouring from a cut on his forearm. 'Look, Sam Lee's man cut me,' he said, staring at the red flow running down the back of his hand.

They tore up their shirts and bandaged the wound. Before they finished, one of the men in charge of their group came up and said, 'It's only a flesh wound. He'll be fine. Get back into your squadron on the hill.'

Peter, who had been wondering how they could manage to slip away and run for home, stared at the man's hostile face and knew what was being said. They would have to stay and fight even if Thomas was wounded. Already too many men had disappeared, the army was shrinking by the hour and the captains would keep the men they had and make them fight, whether they wanted to or not.

And though he was hurt, Thomas was still keen to go to battle. He seemed to sense his brother's thoughts and pulled at his arm urgently. 'Dinna tak' me hame, Peter. I want to see the real King. I want to fight for Jamie,' he said.

There was nothing for it. They would have to stay and go into battle, but more than ever Peter was set on keeping his brother safe. He remembered the kind pikeman and his advice. The thing to do was get hold of pikes and fight with them.

Twenty-Seven

The King and Lady Heron did not emerge from the great chamber for two days. Food and drink were carried in to them, and, unknown to him, information from her was carried out and sent on to Bastard Heron and to the Earl of Surrey, who was hurrying back from Wooler with an army that was growing restive through shortage of supplies, and particularly of ale.

Surrey's men were professional soldiers, and paid to fight, so they were not like James' army, bound to serve for only a certain number of days, but they could not fight well, or with good heart, if they were purging from dysentery through having to drink polluted water. Only ale kept them fighting fit and ale was now practically unobtainable.

It was essential for Surrey to keep to his original schedule. Battle must be joined on 9th September and be over as soon as possible. He had to get his men in position on the date he named in his challenge. Unfortunately James had not agreed to Surrey's choice of place and it was obvious that he intended to make his stand on the top of Flodden Hill, which was a difficult place from the English point of view. If the Scots stayed on the hill, they would have to be attacked time and again but they could fight off their attackers more easily than on flat ground.

In hurried war meetings Surrey listened anxiously to Bastard Heron, who confirmed his own worst fears. 'His army is digging in on Flodden Hill. Even with the men it's losing it's bigger than yours. There's a big contingent of pikemen among them, and pikes are hard to overcome on hill faces. But Jamie's being well delayed in Ford and he's losing focus. If my sister-in-law can keep him there, when he does come out to fight he'll be out of touch. He's a rash man, given to quick decisions, and what you must do is decoy him off that hill. The ground at the bottom is treacherous and he might not know that.'

'Decoy him down. How do you suggest we do that?' asked Dacre sceptically. He was jealous of the way the Bastard was taking over Surrey's ear.

'By sending part of your army up in a northwards direction and then swinging it back round almost to Coldstream. The smaller part can seem to go straight to Coldstream too by crossing the River Till and it's almost unfordable now because the river's running so high. I know one ford that won't be flooded, though, and I can take some mounted men through it. Your foot soldiers will have to go over Twizel Bridge and that'll take a long time because the bridge is so narrow, but it will divert the Scots' attention, especially because they'll be wondering where the soldiers heading north are going – they'll wonder are they're heading for Berwick or Scotland.'

Surrey's son the Lord High Admiral, who always sat in on his father's meetings with the Bastard, who he trusted as little as Dacre did, frowned and said, 'Why will dividing our army bring James off the hill? Won't that weaken us? Why not charge en masse and overrun him from the south?'

The Bastard shook his head. 'If he sees a column of your men marching in the direction of Coldstream, he'll be afraid they're on the way to attack Edinburgh. I'll wager he rushes off the hill to stop them.'

'That's a dangerous wager,' scoffed Dacre.

'Have you a better one?' sneered the cold-eyed Bastard, leaning over the table and staring belligerently at him.

That night another message from Ford Castle arrived for Bastard Heron, who carried it to Surrey and said, 'It seems he's planning to station Home and his men on the west side of the hill, overlooking Coldstream. If they're dug in there, they will see your men and cut them off before the King and the main army is alerted to the danger, so my plan might not work. We'll need to try another tactic as well as the diversion. Leave it to me.'

In the darkness of that night, a ragged man crept over rough boggy land on the south side of the village of Branxton. He wore dark clothes and slipped along the sides of stone walls, moving so quietly that he did not even disturb the few grazing animals that ventured out, though by this time, thanks to soldiers' plundering, most of them were rabbits. All the sheep and cattle for miles around had long ago been stolen and eaten by the Scots.

Cautious as a cur dog, he slipped into the camp, avoiding the sentries sitting round dying fires. There was no moon and the shadows made deep purple caverns that swallowed him up. Lord Home's tent was the biggest of all and his pennant of a green shield with a rampant lion on a black ground drooped from its tallest pole. A lone soldier sat at the tent flap with his legs crossed and his head nodding on his chest. The intruder gently and silently slid the sword that lay by his side away from his hand and then tapped him on the leg with his own dagger.

'Hey, who's that? What do you want?' cried the man, waking with a terrible start.

'I want to speak to Home.'

'Who are you?' The sentry was standing up and searching around for his weapon with one foot.

'Tell him the Bastard has come to pay his respects to him.'

The sentry, like everybody else in the camp, had heard about Bastard Heron and drew back in fear.

'Don't worry. If I wanted to kill you, you'd be a corpse now. Is Home within?'

The answer was a nod. 'Then take me to him and leave your sword here.'

The sound of their voices had woken Home, who was always a light sleeper, and he was sitting up on his stretcher bed with his own dagger in his hand and pointing at the door when the sentry brought in Bastard Heron, who had abandoned his skulking manner and now stood as tall and arrogant as usual.

The two men were old enemies and they stared unsmilingly at each other.

Home spoke first. 'This is a strange time for a neighbourly visit.'

'The last time I called on you, I burned down one of your strongholds at the Hirsel if I remember rightly,' said the Bastard.

'So you did. I had you proscribed for it.'

'I'm in the protection of the Earl of Surrey now, so your Scots writ doesn't matter any more.'

'Does he know he has a cuckoo in his nest?'

'He doesn't trust me any more than Jamie Stewart trusts you, I expect.' Delivering himself of that shot, the Bastard sat down on a stool and said, 'Let's get to business, Home. I have a proposition for you.'

'Knowing you, it won't be a straightforward one.'

'It isn't, but we are not straightforward men, are we? I have an offer to make to you.'

'Well?' The bony face of the man on the bed was very suspicious.

'I hear your men are to hold the slope of Branxton Hill, looking down to Coldstream.'

'How did you learn that? I was only given my orders a few hours ago.'

'This is my country. Even a whisper comes to my ears in time. How committed are you to Jamie?'

'He's my King.'

'So was his father and you looked the other way when they cut his throat. I think that you're like me, more loyal to your own lands than to any ruler.'

There was no reply to that and the Bastard went on, 'I'm with Surrey's army now, but if he loses, I'll be treating with the Scots. You're with James, but if he loses, you won't want the English army tramping over your lands, burning your towers and raping your women.'

There was still no reply. Home was waiting.

'All I ask is for you to stay your hand till you see which side is going to prevail. Surrey will attack Flodden Hill from the north. You'll be on the west. If James stays on the hill, it won't be easy, perhaps not even possible, to dislodge him. Just wait and see what happens before you come rushing in. If James is losing, go home. That way you won't have betrayed anybody, you'll just be saving your men and yourself. No English revenge will fall on you afterwards either. I have Surrey's word for it.'

Home stayed silent, his expression impassive. There was no way of telling what he thought. The Bastard stood up and headed for the tent flap. 'I don't expect you to talk. I'll only know what you think about my offer after the battle is fought, but I know the Home lands are more precious to you than anything else. I think the same way about Ford,' he said.

'You have no possessions. You're base born,' said Home.

'I'm still a Heron and my brother and the Heron lands are as dear to me as my own blood. I'm a survivor too and come what may, I don't intend to suffer over the quarrel of two well-born, vainglorious fools.'

Twenty-Eight

'You are a witch,' James Stewart muttered in Elizabeth Heron's ear. She smiled and twisted in his arms, making it possible to give him greater pleasure in their coupling for she was skilled in the arts of seduction and love-making.

He had never before experienced such prolonged sensual delights and somehow she always managed to spur him on, even when he thought his desire was slaked. He had loved Margaret Drummond but their love-making had always been tender and gentle. Only for her did he remove his brutal chain because he did not want to hurt her, but with this woman cruelty was part of the passion. Even she seemed to appreciate that reason. He wanted to make her scream, and she obliged him many times.

It was as if she wakened the deep, hidden part of him that compelled him to hang the informer at Norham. Margaret would have been horrified by that but Lady Heron understood completely and would have done the same.

They were in their second day of isolation and she had diverted him from even getting up to look out of the tower window. He'd posted no scouts to watch out for the approach of Surrey; he had abandoned himself to her, completely forgetting he'd come to Ford to fight a battle and that his army was drawn up waiting for him just a mile away.

On the third day, he suddenly realized what was being done to him. He was under enchantment. The woman by his side was the Queen of the Fairies, and a malevolent one at that.

He remembered the ballad of Thomas of Ercildoune, which he'd read as a boy. Thomas had been led away by the Fairy Queen and spent what he thought were seven days with her in a cave on the Eildon Hills. When he finally emerged he'd been absent for seven years. She enchanted Thomas just as this woman had spun a magic net around him.

Although he was a man of great learning, there was still a strong streak of superstition in James. Logic told him not to be a fool, but his innermost self believed in magic and witches. When he realized this, he jumped from the bed, threw open the shutters and stared out. Rain was drifting down over the Northumbrian hills again.

'Where's Surrey's army?' he asked her over

his shoulder. She was lying naked in bed, her glorious breasts peaking and pink-nippled like those of a young woman, but suddenly they'd lost their power over him.

'Where's Surrey?' he asked again.

'I have no idea.'

'You're a liar. You know where he is. I realize now that every time food has been brought to us, there was probably some sort of message for you. You've had me enchanted, but your spell's worn off now.'

She got up slowly and pulled a fur-lined cloak over her shoulders.

'You were easy to enchant,' she told him and her tone was icy.

'Why did you do it? Did you truly desire me?' he asked.

She decided to lie. 'Keep him off the field as long as you can,' the Bastard had said in his last message that had been passed to her by a whispering page boy. Her tone was honey sweet when she said, 'Of course I desire you. I still do. Come back to bed.'

But James was pulling on his boots. 'No, my lady. You have had three days of me. I'm due to fight a battle the day after tomorrow. Now I must leave.'

She walked down the stairway with him, resting one hand lightly on his arm as if she was unaware that a rift had opened between them. In the huge inner courtyard some of his men were waiting, and his son Alexander came out of the great hall with her daughter Judith behind him. Judith's face was sullen.

'Fetch my horse,' James said to a servitor, who ran off to the stables.

'Fetch Douglas,' was his next order to one of his men, who ran out of the open gateway, shouting at a group of soldiers encamped beyond the castle moat.

'Would you like to eat before you leave?' Lady Heron asked as if none of this was happening, but he shook his head and kept his eyes fixed on the gate, watching for the approach of his henchman.

When the old man appeared on a huge war horse, he raised his eyebrows enigmatically at the sight of the King but said nothing. 'Is Borthwick still out there?' James asked him.

'He is, but most of his cannons have been hauled away to Flodden.'

'Are there any left trained on this castle?'

'Two are, but the rest of them are on the hill now.'

'Two are sufficient to blow a hole in this place,' said James, and smiled cruelly at Lady Heron, whose expression of calm suddenly changed to one of sheer terror as she cried out, wringing her hands, 'Don't! You can't. You know what Ford means to me. You can't do this...'

'Why not? I'm at war and you are in league with the enemy. But I'm a merciful man. In return for your great hospitality, I won't blast it with my cannons, I'll only burn your castle down. Get your family and retainers out and then I'll put it to the torch.'

She tried to cling to his arm. 'Don't do this, don't!'

He shook her off and issued orders. Within a short time his men were running all through the enormous place, setting fire to piles of brushwood that they stacked against the walls. In moments the dry panelling went up like tinder and screaming servants ran out from all directions, while the lady and her children stood in a close huddle outside the gate staring at orange flames leaping into the sky.

With a sweep of his arm, King James took his leave of her and she raised both fists above her head as she rained curses down on him.

'God damn you, James Stewart. May you burn in Hell. I'll spit on your body soon, you can be sure of that!'

When he looked back at her he was laughing. The wicked spirit that always lurked inside him had taken him over again.

Twenty-Nine

'The Scots are in dismay because the King is behaving as if he is driven by the Devil,' said one of the spies employed by the abbess of Coldstream to bring her all the news from the battlefront. It was generally known that Surrey had challenged James to fight on 9th September and that he'd accepted the challenge. Time was running out but James had only just reappeared among his followers and was acting erratically.

'Perhaps he is driven by the Devil. There's evil in all the Stewarts and also weakness,' she said reflectively. It pained her that all her worst misgivings about the King were being proved right. It was so in character for him to waste precious time with Elizabeth Heron for three days – for everyone knew where he was and what he had been doing – but yet there was so much good in him.

He was magnificently talented and daring; and if he channelled his energies in the right way, he could make Scotland a premier power. He outshone the glutinous Henry Tudor in every way, except for the fatal flaw that ran through him like a fault in a rock.

Though she was a pragmatist, Isabella Hoppringle was a Scot in her soul and James was her king. She paid lip service to serving both countries, but when it came to this conflict her deepest loyalties were to her native land and that was why she sent her most beloved son back to fight.

When she was praying, she sometimes allowed herself the luxury of asking God to protect him, then felt guilty at allowing personal feelings to intrude into her religious duties. Prayers should be sent up for all mankind, not for her own best loved.

She sent off the spy and went wearily into the little hospital and dispensary that was attached to the abbey. There the nuns were busy piling up dressings and ointments for the wounded of both sides in the battle that was surely coming. The abbess watched them and then went out to the gardens, where she ordered the gardeners and lay brothers to equip themselves with as many spades and mattocks as they could find in the town. 'Many graves will have to be dug,' she told them.

As the afternoon drew to its close and the abbey bells started ringing, she walked to the gate and stared over the full, fast-flowing river towards the distant line of hills where the smoke from many camp fires spiralled into the sky. It was 8th September. The last day of life for many men, she feared. God rest their souls.

On the top of the distant hill at which the abbess stared, King James was stamping up and down the floor of his fine tent, watched by his closest associates, whose expressions betrayed deep misgivings about his behaviour.

He had begun the day in high fettle, pausing every now and again to point across at the thick plumes of black smoke rising from Ford Castle and exult, 'That's spiked the power of the Herons. That's what they get for sending a women to try to divert me.'

By afternoon, however, information came in that Lady Heron and her household had managed to douse the fire, though not before it had devastated most of the castle.

'What's left of it?' asked James.

'The great tower, the original keep. She's saved that,' he was told and he knew that the part that remained was the heart of the stronghold, the tower where she had bedded him.

'We'll burn that down too after we've won the battle against Surrey,' he said with bravado when he saw the disapproving expressions on the faces of his companions who knew as well as he did what had gone on in Ford's great tower.

'Where is Surrey now?' he suddenly asked,

in an effort to divert them.

'He's left Wooler. He marched out two days ago,' said one of the Flemings.

'And where is he now, at this minute, where is he?'

No one knew exactly.

'Why did you not send out scouts? You should have people watching him all the time,' James shouted.

They looked at each other and shared the same thought. 'You are the leader of this army. Why did *you* not send out scouts instead of fucking Lady Heron for three days?'

He knew it too and went red in the face as he shouted even louder, 'Are there traitors among you? Are there cowards? Do you not want to fight?'

The Earl of Douglas held up a cautionary hand. 'Your Majesty, perhaps you should consider treating with Surrey. You are in a strong position. He'll deal with you because his army has run out of ale and is short of food. You could win advantages for Scotland by negotiating now ... perhaps he'll even yield Berwick to us. By fighting we are condemning many men to death, even if we prevail.'

James turned on him as if he was a snarling dog. 'If you are afraid to fight, old man, take your soldiers and go away now. You are old and lily livered and I have no need of cowards among my followers. Go! Take your sons and your men and go.'

The old earl bristled with resentment. He had been a loyal supporter of the King ever since he was a boy. 'If I must, I will stay. I have never betrayed you, nor will I, but I think this strategy is ill advised,' he said with dignity.

'I care not what you think, you are doddering in your old age, your brain is addled, why should I pay any attention to your advice?' shouted the King.

Sir Patrick Lindsay, another previously loyal supporter of James, could stand no more of this. 'Fie, my lord,' he said disapprovingly, 'Douglas is your man through and through. There is no need to insult or shame him. You are distraught. Perhaps it would be best if you did not take part in this coming battle.'

James reacted as if he did not believe what he was hearing. 'Say that again,' he ordered.

'Perhaps it would be best if Your Majesty did not take part in the fighting, but stayed safe behind the lines while the rest of us fight it out,' said Lindsay calmly.

'You are mad,' yelled James.

'I am not mad. I see no reason why you should risk your life. You have only one son and he is still an infant. If you were to be killed, who would rule Scotland?'

Other men in the gathering made sounds of agreement. 'Listen to Lindsay,' said some of them, because, like him, they were beginning to feel that James's impulsive and uncontrolled behaviour was making him more of a liability than an asset.

'I have a good son here,' said James, pointing at Alexander.

'He cannot be an archbishop and a king,' interjected Douglas, who thought little of Alexander.

'Besides, he's a bastard,' said Lindsay.

As he said this, he looked round at the faces of his companions and saw agreement there. One or two of them nodded. James saw that too and it seemed to drive him beyond reason.

'Seize him, hang him,' he yelled pointing at Lindsay.

A couple of men stepped forward to obey his orders, but others standing beside them held them back and nothing happened.

'I want you hanged,' the King hissed at his one-time friend, who stared stonily back at him.

'Hang him, hang him!' Losing control, James rushed forward shouting and tried to loop a belt round Lindsay's neck. One of the younger Douglas sons stepped between them and said soothingly, 'Your Majesty, Sir Patrick will apologize to you. He did not mean to demean you or cast doubt on your ability as a fighter.' With a hard look at Lindsay, he added, 'Say it.'

'I regret if I caused pain to my monarch,' said Lindsay stonily.

'Get out of my sight. If I ever see you again, I *will* hang you,' James told him.

The other lords watched Lindsay go. Many of them sympathized and agreed with him but they knew the die was cast.

Thirty

Tomorrow we fight...
As darkness fell that was the thought uppermost in the mind of every man in both armies.

Thousands of men with one predominating thought.

The question that struck them next was, 'Will I still be alive at this time tomorrow?' but few of them said it aloud.

They huddled round guttering fires, for it was still drizzling, and stared into the embers as if they were trying to read their futures.

They passed round bottles they'd been saving for this very day and many of the Highlanders started singing strange songs in their own language that sounded like dirges, blood-chilling and melancholy as death chants.

Friends and brothers sat together, huddled under shared blankets for warmth in the chilly night, and tried to divert each other by gossiping or talking about the past. Some gave each other messages to be passed on to their loved ones if they were killed.

'Tell Mary the old horse'll be good for another year or two...' 'Tell my mother I've left a wee pot of money hidden in the chimney piece above the bread oven...' 'Tell my lassie I love her...' All of them thought about people they loved or had loved, wives, parents, children or sweethearts.

The Fletcher brothers talked about Selkirk, remembering people from their childhood and telling each other old jokes. When their fire began burning out, Robert suddenly rose, then sank to his knees and raised his hands in prayer. 'God take care of us all. Let us see our home town again,' he said fervently. His brothers bent their heads around him and some reached for a brother's shoulder and squeezed it hard.

Sam Lee spent the evening trying to find his brothers. When the King came back from Ford, his position as a valued decoy was no longer needed. In a pitched battle, it would only cause trouble if the army began following two kings. Lord Home did not waste words of thanks on Sam, but ordered him to strip off his glorious clothes and get back into his leather jerkin and remove himself. Knowing better than to argue, Sam went, but not before he slipped into his deep poacher's pocket a fine golden necklet he'd been wearing when he masqueraded as James.

His search for his brothers proved fruitless because they were behind the lines, making sure that the horses on which they intended to make their escape after the battle were safely tied up where they would easily find them, and the finest saddlery they could lay their hands on was hidden nearby as well.

In his wanderings from group to group, Sam eventually chanced upon the Purvis brothers and Sandy Hogg, who still had some bread left from the supplies Lucy gave them. Sandy was cutting them each a slice when Lee sat down beside them and said, 'What about a slice for your old neighbour?'

'Didn't they feed you when you were parading around dressed like a lord?' asked Peter.

'Not them. Home's a greedy infidel,' said Sam, reaching over and cutting a slice for himself.

'Where's your braw clothes?' asked Thomas.

'All gone, except for this,' was the reply as Sam pulled the fine chain out of his pocket and slipped it over his head.

'You stole that, of course,' said Peter but Sam only laughed and said, 'Why not? And I'm making sure nobody steals it off me,' as he slid the chain under his dirty shirt and tied a rag round his neck to hide it.

To Peter's dismay their unwanted companion seemed intent on staying with them, and he settled down at their fire and started to advise them on how to behave in the coming battle. 'You stay with me. I'll look after you. First we'll get ourselves some good horses and load them up with booty before we head for home. I'll show you what to take.'

'How'll we be able to take booty when there's a battle going on?' asked Sandy.

Sam laughed. 'If you stick with me, we won't be doing much fighting. I know how to keep out of trouble.'

He was interrupted by a quartermaster who was going up the lines passing out rations of ale to help put the men to sleep, but in spite of it many lay open-eyed staring into the blackness and wondering if a black, bottomless void was all that awaited them in death.

They lay silently praying, mentally checking their arms, and wondering where the enemy were and when the fighting would start.

Thirty-One

Friday, 9th September

Lucy, sleeping on top of the food cart, dreamt that she was at home in the mill and the grassy bank behind the house was spangled with primroses. She opened her eyes and saw the two old men who had looked after her standing together at the cart wheel, heads together and faces solemn. She lay still because she knew they were discussing the best way to save themselves – and her – if the worst happened.

Dawn was breaking in silvery streaks across a dark grey sky. A late-summer sun was struggling through the rain clouds which were still massed over the Northumbrian hills. Towards the east, curls of smoke still rose from the burned-out Ford Castle.

On Flodden Hill the men of the Scottish army were waking up, stretching, relieving themselves in coppices, making jokes, exchanging insults, grumbling.

Lucy sat up in the cart and Willie looked round towards her. 'You're wakened, lass?

Come doon. There's something we want to tell ye,' he said.

She clambered out of her oat-sack bed and went to join them.

'This'll no' be a place for a lassie when the English arrive. We've got you a horse and we want you to get yourself as far away as you can before the killing starts,' said Old Tom.

'But what about my brothers? I can't go away and leave them,' she said.

Tom shook his head. 'They'll hae to take their chance like a'body else. The horse is tied up over there in that old byre, we picked you a good yin. Get on its back and go home if you can. Willie's been watching it all night in case somebody else has the same idea.'

She sobbed, 'I can't go away and leave my brothers here.'

Tom shook his head. 'You'll be well oot o' it. Staying here won't help your brothers. A battle's no' a place for a lassie unless she's one o' the body robbers and you're not that.'

'Body robbers?' she asked.

He gestured towards the place where the women who followed the army had set up their rough camp. 'They'll move in and strip the bodies as soon as the killing starts, and it will, it will.'

She shuddered as the horror of what was about to happen struck her. They saw she was upset and Willie pressed his advantage. 'Get on the horse and clear off. We dinna want to see you get into trouble. If you think you have to stay till it's all over, go to the nuns at Coldstream. They'll move in after the fighting but they'll help the wounded and bury the dead. People say the abbess has everything ready. If you don't want to go home yet, go and help her, then you'll find out what happens to your brothers and be safe at the same time.'

Old Tom shook his head as he disagreed with his friend. 'It'd be better if the lassie gets on the horse and goes straight home. She disnae want to see the things the nuns'll see this day.'

To Lucy he said, 'Head south and turn west to Yetholm when you see the big Cheviot. Dinna stop for anybody. The horse we got you is fast. It'll outrun anything.'

She looked from wrinkled face to wrinkled face and saw the concern and kindness there. Throwing her arms round them, she said, 'You've been so good to me. I don't want to leave you. Will you have to fight too? How will you get away?'

Willie laughed. 'There'll be no fighting for us. We're old hands and we know how to take to our heels when things are bad. Come on lass, dinna argue and dinna worry aboot us. Come and let me see you get on that horse's back.'

She knew they were right and it was point-less to argue, so she went with them into a tumbledown farm shed where a fine chestnut mare stood tied up to the central post. She wore a fine bridle with silver mountings but no saddle though there was a blanket thrown over her back. When she saw people, she rolled her eyes and blew loudly through her nostrils. The tension that filled everybody in the army seemed to have affected even a horse.

'Can you ride without a saddle?' Willie asked Lucy and she nodded.

He held out his cupped hands for her foot and said, 'Then get up and I'll lead you out.'

Tears filled her eyes when she was perched on the mare's shivering back. 'Thank you both so much, but how will I find you again when this is all over?' she said as she gathered up the reins.

'Just ask in Kelsae. A'body there kens us,' was Willie's reply as he led the mare through the open shed door, gave it a sharp slap on the rump and stood with his arms crossed as it took off with a huge leap, almost dislodging Lucy. 'Hing on, hing on,' were the last words she heard as she rode away.

But she had made up her mind and had no intention of going home yet. Peter and Thomas could not be abandoned now, for she had originally set out to find them. She could not go home without her brothers. She must stay to find out how they fared in the battle.

Besides, she'd come so far with the army that she felt part of it and must see the adventure through to the end, even if only from the sidelines. She was seventeen, an age when people thought that bad things happened to other people, but never to themselves.

The chestnut mare, relieved to be out of the stable, galloped like the wind and it would have been difficult to stop it even if Lucy wanted to do so. They headed south, across high moors and over stone walls, till the big Cheviot rose up on the horizon. At that point Lucy did manage to draw rein and, instead of turning westwards for the safety of the village of Yetholm, she doubled back towards Coldstream.

Approaching the ford from the western side she saw men working on both banks, still laying a foundation of straw bales on the river floor to make the crossing easier. Rain was still falling and the Tweed was running high.

A group of nuns huddled on the far bank watching the work, and one of them beckoned to her when she reined in her horse.

'Where are you going, boy? Have you a message for the abbess?' the woman shouted.

'I've come to help,' Lucy called back, surprised at being taken for a boy again.

'Bring him over,' the nun called to one of

the labourers, who took hold of her horse's bridle and guided it onto the ford. The water level was so high that it swirled round her calves but the mare fought on gallantly and soon emerged on the northern back, shaking itself vigorously.

The nuns were watching her suspiciously. The tallest of them asked, 'What can a boy like you do to help? Are you a runaway? Are you English or Scots?'

Lucy sat on her horse and stared them out. 'I'm not a boy, I'm a girl, and I'm from Scotland. I want to stay and help you till the battle is over because my brothers are in the King's army and they'll have to cross this ford on their way home, won't they?'

A haughty-looking woman, wearing a beautiful jewelled cross on her breast, came walking down the slope and the other nuns fell back in front of her. She stared unsmiling at Lucy and asked, 'What sort of help can you give?'

'I heard that you will help the wounded after the battle. I want to find my brothers, you see...'

The abbess did not soften and still looked suspicious. 'Decent girls don't follow armies. Are you a whore?'

'Of course not!'

'Then what are you doing here?'

Lucy grimaced. 'I've been foolish. I thought it was unfair that boys could join the

King's army and I couldn't ... I didn't realize what it was like, you see...'

'So you tagged along?' There was a slight note of understanding in the abbess's voice. 'That's a good horse you're riding. Did you steal it?' was what she asked next, however.

Lucy was indignant again. 'No, I did not. It was given to me. Can I stay and help you? I'm very willing.'

Her persistence impressed the abbess, who looked at the ragged little person with a slight softening of her expression. 'Very well. Put your horse in our stables. When the killing starts we'll need all the help we can get, but don't start fainting or weeping or feeling sick at the sight of blood because there'll be plenty of that today. Do you understand?'

'Yes, I understand,' said Lucy grimly and thought she was telling the truth. In a very short time, however, she was to find out that whatever she imagined was only a faint version of the terrible reality.

Thirty-Two

Surrey's army was heading north, unhampered and unharried. They spent the night before the battle encamped at Barmoor Wood not far from where James' army was digging in on Flodden Hill, and Surrey sat in his tent revising his tactics with his son and his advisers.

He felt old and ill. He wished with all his heart that this terrible enterprise was over. Death would be a relief but he was a loyal servant of the crown and would do his duty to the end. Outside his tent flap he saw that rain was still pouring down. His archers would not be so effective in such weather because too much rain slackened their bow strings.

He groaned and his son leaned solicitously towards him and asked what was wrong.

'Everything is wrong. This whole campaign is wrong. If James Stewart had any sense he'd have treated with us. Queen Catherine would have ceded Berwick to him. What more does he think he's fighting for?'

Thomas Howard, Surrey's son, grimaced.

'He's hungry for glory. He thinks he's one of Arthur's knights. He won't withdraw without a battle.'

Surrey nodded his head. 'At least we have God on our side. We're carrying St Cuthbert's banner from Durham.'

His son clapped him on the shoulder. 'That's a consolation,' he agreed, though he had less confidence than his father in the power of a strip of old cloth. He was relying on the accuracy of his archers.

What annoyed Howard most of all was the continual braggart presence of Bastard Heron, who swaggered around in the middle of a pack of thieves like himself, telling whoever would listen that he had secret knowledge that would swing the battle England's way. Exactly what that was, he never revealed and Howard suspected him of double-dealing, because he wouldn't put it past the villain to be bargaining with the Scots for a pardon in the same way as he was dealing with his father. After all, he was proscribed by both sides and so had nothing to lose, for wasn't he one of the most dangerous of the renegade lords of the Debatable Lands? Among them, none was more debatable than the Herons, who owed allegiance to no one but themselves.

Howard watched while the man he so distrusted leaned over his father's shoulder and whispered in his ear. It had to be admitted that there was a change in the Bastard's attitude since he heard how James burned down Ford Castle. He seemed to be more intent on defeating the Scots than ever before. Had he finally chosen sides?

Surrey looked up and caught his son's eye. 'He insists we split our army in two, half to march north-west to Twizel Bridge and pretend they're heading into Scotland. He'll guide the other half over the bog at Pallinsburn.'

'Pallinsburn bog is said to be bottomless. No army can cross it,' spluttered Dacre.

The Bastard swung round and sneered at him. 'That's all you know. There's a causeway over the bog and it leads to Branxton...'

Dacre appealed to Surrey. 'He's going to lead our men into the bog and let them sink.'

The outlaw had an answer for that too. 'This is my calf country. I know the causeway. I've crossed it in worse weather than this. Give me some men and we'll line up along the edges so no man strays off the path. Trust me...' This was directed at Surrey.

Howard asked, 'Why split our army up?'

The Bastard replied, 'I've told you already, when James' scouts see them at Twizel, they'll think we're heading for Berwick. The bog is in a hollow with thick scrub all over it. He won't see us in there till we are on him, and he won't think we'll try crossing it anyway. He'll chase after the men heading north and that'll be a way of luring him off Branxton Hill.'

'And what if he doesn't bite?' asked Dacre.

'We circle round and come back at him from the north, while the rest of the force attacks from the east. I want to beat him as much as you do,' said the Bastard, looking hard into Surrey's face. Suddenly the other man knew that, for once at least, the outlaw was telling the truth.

'All right ... go ahead. We've nothing to lose. We're hopelessly outnumbered anyway,' he reluctantly agreed.

At nine o'clock that morning he was helped onto the top of a cart and addressed his army. Terrible pity for those about to die filled him as he gazed over the sea of faces, grim beneath steel helmets, and exhorted them, 'Today we join with the Scots in battle. I want you all to fight like Englishmen, like heroes. God be with you!'

A tremendous cheer roared up as he climbed down and started to don his own armour. Even at his age he was not going to stay back from the fighting. He would be in the middle of it with his men and leading the contingent to Twizel Bridge.

His son proudly settled a crested helmet on his head and then heaved him up into the saddle of his war horse while the soldiers

cheered him again. Father and son held
hands for a few moments and blessed each
other, not knowing if either of them would
live to see the sun set that night.

Thirty-Three

In the Scottish army on Flodden Hill overlooking Branxton village, activity started at
the same time as it did among the enemy.
Men shivered in the rain and cursed the
weather, which had stayed wet and dreary
for a whole week.

When they looked up at the sky in hope of
spotting a break in the clouds, a pale sun
suddenly tried to break through and a mild
cheer ran through the ranks, but immediately it was followed by a shocked silence.

Men looking up at the cluster of tents on
the top of the hill where the King's special
pavilion was erected gasped in horror, because they saw that the tent was glowing red.
It looked as if it was dripping blood.

Nobleman and foot soldier alike stared at it
in superstitious horror. 'Is it an omen?' they
asked each other. What they did not realize
was that the scarlet-flounced trimmings
along the edges of the roof had leached dye

in the morning dew and stained the canvas so that it looked as if it was drenched in gore.

Men sank to their knees in fear of death and the more superstitious scrabbled with their hands in the wet earth, stuffing soil into their mouths as if they were eating the sacrament at mass.

As they were praying, the King emerged into the light, dressed in glorious colours, gleaming like a god. Even the most fearful felt that it was impossible for such a magnificent leader to be defeated.

'Where are the English?' he asked his son, and the question was passed from man to man.

'Where are they?' he asked again. 'Surrey challenged me to fight today, the ninth of September. Has he run away? Is he going to avoid his own challenge?'

The Archbishop of St Andrews laughed as if his father had made a joke. 'He's not here, so he must be afraid of you,' he said. They turned and stared to the east but not a man could be seen.

'We must wait to find if he has the stomach for a battle,' said James scornfully, waving a hand for his war horse to be led up. Springing into the saddle, he stared down at his son and his closest supporters and it did not escape his notice that some of the faces were very grim and apprehensive.

What cravens! They're afraid I might lose!

he realized, and he set out to ride round the lines, waving, smiling and encouraging his soldiers.

The disquiet was not confined to noblemen, however, and wild rumours of all kinds were running through the ranks. The chief of them was that Surrey was marching away, and this gained currency when a scout came charging in to tell the King that Surrey's army might be heading for Twizel Bridge.

'Twizel Bridge! Once he crosses that, the way is open for him to march into Scotland. All the Scots are gathered at Flodden. There will be no one to stop his progress,' said the doubters.

These speculations especially alarmed some of the depleted Edinburgh contingent, who took the opportunity to slip away themselves, taking their blue blanket banner with them. They consoled themselves with the observation that if what they heard was true, they would be more needed at home when Surrey besieged their city than they would be on Flodden Hill. They rode north fast and when they arrived home they gave orders to the other citizens to start building a huge wall round their city. Only the provost and a handful of loyal burgesses stayed to fight.

Time dragged on and every man in the waiting army felt as if he was in the grip of a suspension of life. Some were agonized by indecision, others, more stoic, resigned themselves to whatever lay ahead. They sat waiting, waiting, waiting … holding their breath, hardly daring to think, eyes darting in every direction, alert to every movement, ears open to every shout.

Many of them jumped to their feet and grabbed their weapons as another rider appeared shouting, 'Surrey's going to Berwick.'

When he heard this, the King, who had returned to his scarlet tent, asked his close advisers, the earls of Cassilis, Morton and Rothes, 'Is he giving up? Does it mean he's backing off? Will he take ship from Berwick and sail away?'

Cassilis shook his head. 'Who knows? If he's in retreat we should chase him.'

But the Earl of Morton disagreed. 'No, no. That might be what he wants. How do we know we wouldn't be riding into an ambush? We're not sure all his army is heading north. It wouldn't be good tactics for him to send fifteen thousand men over Twizel Bridge, because it is very narrow. We should stay here and watch till we know more about where all the English are.'

'Surely someone knows if he's heading for Cornhill or Berwick?' Cassilis asked the scout. He was furious at James for not having set up a network of scouts.

'But why should Surrey take his army to Twizel? If he's not leaving, he could come to us here by crossing the river at Mill Ford. He wouldn't need to go as far as the bridge.' James was puzzled. Only now did he realize the magnitude of his mistake in not keeping a closer eye on the activities of the English.

In the crowd of anxious men now surrounding the King there was a grave-looking fellow called Giles Musgrave, an English-born gallant of the court and husband to one of Queen Margaret's ladies. He caught the King's eye and grimaced as the news of Surrey's army's movements were being discussed.

'What are you thinking, Musgrave?' James asked.

'I fear Surrey's main army is off to raid the Berwickshire Merse and won't come here to fight at all,' said Musgrave.

James stared back, momentarily indecisive, for what Musgrave said was exactly what he feared himself. It would be a cunning move.

What to do? Chase Surrey or sit tight? His instinct was to chase, to remount his horse and charge off in pursuit, but there was something in Musgrave's face that made him pause. He remembered that the man was English-born though he had been in the Scottish court for ten years because he came north with Queen Margaret from England.

Where did his loyalties lie? Was it possible that he had been in communication with fellow Englishmen in the other camp? The armies were so close, it was impossible to stop people secretly slipping back and forwards.

For once James decided on caution, but he smiled and said graciously, 'Thank you for your counsel, Musgrave, but I think we should stay where we are. Home's army is on our west side, nearer the ford at Coldstream, and, if Surrey is off to raid in Berwickshire, Home will ride after him. Those are his lands, after all.'

He also made up his mind to give an instruction to one of his bodyguards to kill Musgrave as soon as the fighting started. If he had been trying to influence events on Surrey's behalf, it was only what he deserved.

Just then a third scout rode in, shouting out more disturbing news of Surrey's deployment: 'There are armed men very near – at Pallinsburn!'

Pallinsburn was just over a mile away and no one could believe that the first of the English forces had crossed a reputedly bottomless bog.

It was already noon. The morning had slipped away in speculation and apprehension, but now the English soldiers were drawing near, and it was time for the fighting to start.

James eagerly jumped up and clapped his favourites on the back. He felt as if his head had miraculously cleared and he was in charge of his destiny. His son fetched up his fighting armour and he felt his body go taut and as tightly sprung as a bow string.

Then, to his irritation, he realized that the chain round his waist had begun to irk him. His exertions with Lady Heron had created an area of intense irritation and broken the skin on his left side. He put a hand on it and thought he had to get rid of the pain before he went into battle. Nothing must distract him when the fighting began.

Though he'd told Lady Heron that he could not remove the chain, it was a lie for a clever smith had created an ingenious invisibly hinged link, which could be opened. Gesturing to St Andrews to withdraw deeper inside the tent with him, he pulled up his surcoat and showed his son the flaming red patch.

'It looks sore,' said the young man.

'It is sore. Help me loosen it.'

'Are you going to take it off?' The idea appalled St Andrews, because he knew his father wore it all the time. If he took it off today, that would be a bad omen.

'Of course not. It is a pledge to St Ninian and I need his protection today of all days. Help me loosen the link.'

When the chain swung loose, he sliced a ribbon off one of the puffed sleeves of his padded doublet and tied the two metal ends together, then tucked it safely into his tight waistband so that it would no longer chafe him. No matter how much he turned and twisted, it must not fall off, because he dreaded losing it.

'When the fighting is over, I'll have a smith make another link and join it up again,' he told his son.

As he strode fully caparisoned back into the body of the tent, Robert Borthwick, his master of ordnance, was waiting for him.

He felt comforted by the sight of the tall, grizzled man who had campaigned and travelled all over Europe, and was respected far beyond Scotland's boundaries for his expertise. James knew that Borthwick had been the engineer of all his victories so far.

'Are our guns in position, old friend?' he asked in a man-to-man voice.

Borthwick nodded shortly. He never crawled to the King, always speaking to him as an equal, and now he said, 'Aye, they're ready, Jamie. We're more than equal to any ordnance Surrey has. Our cannonry is heavier and has a longer range. Our cannonballs are twice the size of his as well. The English are firing peas compared to the balls we have.'

The King laughed and clapped him on his shoulder, saying, 'Good. Where are our guns dug in?'

'On the face of this hill, halfway up.'

'Why not on the top?'

'Halfway up is best. If we were up too high our cannonballs would only go over their heads as they advance. From where we are, we'll shoot right into them.'

'That's good.'

Borthwick frowned slightly. 'Let's hope so, anyway. We'll only know for sure when the fighting starts. Where is he? I hope he doesn't keep us waiting too long.'

Lower down the hill from the King's tent, huge bonfires of brushwood and rubbish had been piled up waiting to be fired and make a smokescreen so the attackers could not see where the Scots were lined up. For half an hour, the King and his courtiers stood on the raised ground straining their eyes towards Pallinsburn.

Suddenly a small group of mounted men emerged from the scrub of the moss and the King yelled out, 'This is it! Light the bonfires!'

Torches were set to the huge piles and flames soared into the air. Curling plumes of thick grey smoke from the wet wood drifted out of the heart of the piles and down over the low land and marshes at the bottom of the hill.

The smell wakened nostalgic memories of wood fires in their homes in the tense waiting men. The small posse who first appeared in the valley were obscured by the smoke and as far as the watchers could see there were no more soldiers coming out of the bog.

In fact the Bastard was waiting for the smoke to clear a little before he made the first attack. In a plain leather jerkin and a steel bonnet, he waited and waited, saying nothing to anyone, staring fixedly ahead of him, his face set. The Bastard was the only man in the group who did not mutter prayers to himself.

As the afternoon drew on, the Scots on the top of the hill found the waiting hard to endure. Some of the cooler men started to play dice while the more devout prayed. The Highlanders sang their mournful songs and drank the last of the strong liquor they'd brought with them and had been saving in their horn flasks for the final battle. Others huddled together and discussed the omens they imagined were all around them, especially the warning of the King's red tent.

Among the Borderers under the command of Lord Home, the Fletcher brothers from Selkirk sat in a group, saying little, staring out over the dismal, smoke-wreathed ground. Near them were a group from Hawick, many of whom they knew. Some strained their eyes in an effort to catch a last sight of the Eildons, those magical, magnetic hills that seemed to draw people towards them by some irresistible force.

The Purvis brothers leaned together in the shadow of a huge cannon with their friend Sandy, and Peter tried to comfort his whimpering younger brother whose arm, still in its bloody bandages, was being held away from his body as if it hurt him.

'What's the matter, Thomas? Does your arm hurt?' he asked.

'A wee bit, but I'm sad about Lucy.'

'I am too. I hope she gets away before the fighting starts,' Peter said.

'She's no' the running kind,' said Sandy.

'That's what's troubling me,' agreed Peter.

'And I want to see the King, the real King, no' Sam Lee,' went on Thomas mournfully.

'I've a feeling you'll see him soon enough,' Sandy told him, and Thomas sighed. 'That'd be grand,' he said.

'It's a good thing somebody's happy,' was Sandy's rejoinder, for he was tired of the enterprise and only wanted to go home. His mother had given him a lucky rabbit's foot to carry in his pocket and now he gently stroked its fur with one finger in an attempt to bring himself good luck.

King James had no time for sitting around thinking about good-luck omens. On his huge war horse, as magnificent as an emperor in glorious tabard, fine armour and glittering jewellery, he patrolled his army, always conscious of the need for display and to show himself as 'a very parfit gentil knight', a hero of legend.

Midday was long past and there was still no sign of Surrey. James, besieged by requests for favours from his closest supporters, promised again that there would be no death tax payable on any of their estates if they were killed. This was a huge concession, because death tax from great landowners was an enormous, and much resented, source of revenue for the crown.

He also granted pardons to men who had been banished from court for one misdemeanour or other, even to Sir William Sinclair of Caithness, who had long been out of royal favour. His pardon was scrawled by the King on the skin of a drum because the monkish scribes had removed themselves from the scene of danger and were now watching from a safe distance.

A regular stream of scouts started to ride into the camp bringing news of the location of Surrey's army, which they said was slowly advancing from the south-east; but no one was sure where Howard's men had gone – were they advancing into Scotland, or were they going to Berwick to embark and run away, as some hopefuls predicted? What was more worrying was the possibility they were heading for Edinburgh to sack the city.

As the tension rose, the King's coolness increased and his close associates regarded him with admiration as he conversed easily with them while one of his servants trimmed his beard so that the ties of his helmet would not become entangled in it. It was the first time any of them had seen him almost clean shaved and they were struck by his handsomeness and the nobility of his features. Without the beard he looked younger than his forty years.

He laughed as long, curly strands of reddish-black hair fell around his feet. 'I was proud of that beard. It's taken years to grow,' he said.

'Rather no beard than no helmet, and then no head,' joked one of the sons of Wedderburn.

'Indeed,' agreed James, setting a be-ringed hand on the man's steel-covered arm.

Another servant passed him a goblet with semiprecious stones set around its brim, and he sipped at the wine carelessly, setting it down at his feet when a glimmer of faint sunlight suddenly broke through the clouds. Its flitting light lit the material of the tent again and sent a sheen of scarlet over his face, which made the more superstitious among the crowd shiver and once more draw back in dread.

That dread was intensified when a hare suddenly dashed through the tent flap. A dog was chasing it, but one of the guards grabbed the dog's collar as it passed him and held it back. Panic-stricken, the hare kept running, right up to the King's feet where it fell dead of exhaustion, its sides heaving as it drew its last breath.

A chill fell over the crowd. This was another dreadful omen. James felt their disquiet and tried to defuse the situation by poking at the hare's corpse with a booted toe and saying casually to a servant, 'Take it away. It'll be my supper after we've won the battle...'

Some men managed to smile at this sally but it struck a chill in many hearts.

Minutes seemed like hours and they ticked past so slowly that men could hear their own hearts beating. Time crept on. Soon it would be evening. Where was Surrey? Where was Howard? Where were the men who came out of the bog?

They were certainly coming, but when?

While they waited, knowing that their ends might be near, men of all ranks once more knelt on the ground and took a handful of earth, putting it into their mouths as their last communion. At least they would die shriven.

Thirty-Four

Suspense ended in mid-afternoon when frenzied shouting was heard from the west. 'A Home! A Gordon!' came cries which told the other waiting Scots soldiers that Home's army had at last engaged the enemy. Howard's men had circled round from the west and to attack the western hill on which Home waited. At last the battle was on!

Some seven thousand Border men, who shouted for Home, were fighting shoulder to shoulder with three thousand Aberdeenshire Highlanders, led by the Earl of Huntly, whose battle cry was 'A Gordon!'

Their force outnumbered the English by almost twenty to one, but the Borderers were at a disadvantage on foot because they normally fought on horseback carrying lances or swords. Only the leaders in charge of the fighting were mounted. For this fight the foot soldiers were equipped with pikes supplied by their French allies, but they found them hard to handle, having had no previous training with the weapon.

The English were far better armed and

armoured and their professional archers claimed a terrible toll among the closely ranked amateur pikemen who were massed together in circular groups and stood their ground with their eighteen-foot pikes stuck straight out so that they looked from a distance like gigantic hedgehogs.

While they held together, it was almost impossible for the English attackers to occupy the hill on which they stood, but when accurately aimed arrows rained down on them, and men started to fall, the hedgehogs fragmented and the battle became a frenzied hand-to-hand scrap with daggers or bill-hooks instead of pikes.

It was fast and bloody, with many casualties on both sides, but no one had time to stop and take a count. They swayed to and fro, up and down the slopes of the hill, with men shouting and screaming as they hacked at each other. The Scots refused to give ground, and Howard could make no headway.

'Those Border men know how to fight,' he gasped when he realized that his force was in danger of being overrun if not annihilated.

He needed help, so he dragged a gold badge from round his neck, gave it to a rider by his side and said, 'Take this to my father. Tell him to come to the aid of his son.'

While he waited for backup, he withdrew his force to the bottom of the hill and the battered men on the hill top paused to take account of what had happened to them. The whole thing had lasted less then ten minutes but on the Scots side some five thousand men were dead, and corpses of English casualties sprawled on the grass below them.

Miraculously Peter and Thomas were alive but deeply shocked, especially Peter, who had run his pike through a charging Englishman and knew he would remember the man's contorting face as he died for the rest of his life.

The men from Selkirk gathered together and counted their losses. They had been in the middle of the melee and thirty-five of them were dead. Robert Fletcher counted heads. So many gone and this terrible battle was not finished yet. 'What's God thinking about?' he groaned to the brother by his side.

James' army on the farther side of the hill was watching the first engagement, and when he saw Howard's men retreating, Borthwick turned to the King to say, 'If they draw back far enough from Home's men, I'll fire on them. That'll break them up completely and end this quickly in our favour.'

To his surprise and disapproval, James dissented and shook his head. 'No. You can't do that. It is not chivalrous to fire on men who are retreating,' he said.

'What? What? Have you lost your senses?'

shouted Borthwick angrily, forgetting the courtesies paid to a king. 'This is *war*, sire. It's not a joust. Forget your notions of chivalry. Howard would fire on us in the same position, I'm sure of that.'

Just as angry, James turned on him. 'I'll never forget about chivalry and I order you, Borthwick, not to fire.'

The master of ordnance spat on the ground, turned on his heel and strode furiously away. He dare not countermand the King's orders though he knew they were wrong-headed.

In fact it was a deadly mistake.

James did not have long to think about this first disagreement between him and his most valuable commander, for within minutes the main body of Surrey's troops came over a little rise at the foot of Branxton Hill. Like wraiths they suddenly appeared through the smoke.

Guided by the Bastard over land that James thought to be impassable, they materialized, marching in close array, well organized by professional soldiers. From the Scots' viewpoint on top of the hill they looked like a massive horde fronted by lines of archers, who kneeled in firing positions and let loose a torrent of arrows. On each side of them were the English cannons, which started to roar at the same time.

Even from the distance it was possible to see Surrey's standard. James' eyes were sharp and he pointed out his enemy to the men beside him, 'There's Surrey on the white horse. I want to kill him myself. No one else must do it. Surrey's blood has to be cast by me.'

When the shouting and yelling began again on the far end of the hill, Thomas asked his brother, 'Are they coming back?' Peter looked down the slope and saw another onslaught of attacking Englishmen.

'I'm afraid they are, but stay alongside me. Don't leave my side, no matter what happens.'

Their friend Sandy pushed his way through groups of stunned and apprehensive men to say, 'You're safe. That's good. My brothers are safe too but two Lees are gone and so's your cousin, the one frae Dryburgh.'

'Aw, poor Robbie. I'm feart. Can we no' go home now?' Thomas asked.

'No, not yet, Tom. It wouldn't be safe to try to get to Coldstream now. The English are picking off anybody that comes off this hill, so we're safer up here and hope that none of them get at us,' said Peter.

'I've got my eye on Home. He's on the top of that hill over there, watching what's going on. When he takes to his heels, I'll do the same,' said cautious Sandy.

He pointed at the dwarfish figure of the

man who was their leader, perched on his huge war horse staring bleakly across the field of battle. What was he waiting for?

In fact he was staring down at Dacre, who he knew well, for the Border was a moveable frontier and they had often fought in local battles – on the same side. When Howard joined up with his father, Dacre and his men were sent to reinforce the troops about to attack Home again. Many of the men fighting under his banner, knew, or were even related to, men they saw on Dacre's. A kind of desperate madness had seized them all. No matter if it was a blood relative or a friend who was rushing at you with his sword raised, the only thing to do was kill or be killed.

The second onslaught against Home's men was almost as bloody as the first, but again they fought valiantly and held their position, and soon the English drew back once more to regroup. Once again the hillside was covered with dead or dying men whose terrible groans made the survivors shudder in horror.

'If they were animals it would be kind to kill them now,' muttered Robert Fletcher as he went among mangled bodies, searching for his brothers and any survivors among the Selkirk men who had ridden out of his home town with him.

He found Dan, dead and horribly injured

with one of his arms completely severed. Robert wept and knelt by his brother's side trying to close his staring eyes. When he wiped the tears off his cheeks he did not realize that he had streaked his face with his brother's blood.

Suddenly a roar of cannonry came from the eastern side of the hill. Scottish guns retaliated at once, splitting the air and sending flashes of flame into the grey afternoon. By four o'clock the whole ridge and both ends of the hill had turned into an inferno of firing cannons and fighting men.

The fateful Battle of Flodden was well and truly underway now.

The two wings of the English force now formed into one and some of the survivors of Home's men ran towards the King's force, where they could see they were badly needed.

In the confusion, two mounted men met in the lee of the western hill. One man wore Dacre's livery and the other was a Home. A few words were exchanged before they parted and a few minutes later Dacre's force wheeled about to rejoin Howard while Home sat unmoving among a group of his closest supporters, watching the valley below.

He was waiting to see how the battle would go and his midnight conversation with Bastard Heron was prominent in his mind.

On top of the eastern side of Branxton Heights, James was going mad with impatience. He wanted to fight, to wield his sword, to kill. Impatient by nature, he longed to be in the middle of a fight but the English cannons were still barking out their messages of death into the Scots' lines and well-drilled archers were loosing off their shafts with devastating accuracy. It was not the time to rush in among the enemy. Each time there was another roar of artillery, his horse reared and he raised his arm jubilantly as if in a cheer. His jubilance disappeared however when a blood-splattered messenger galloped up to him and gasped, 'Bad news, sire, it's Borthwick.'

'Borthwick? My cannon master? What's happened to him?' asked the King.

'He's dead. A blast from one of the English guns got him.'

James groaned. Sir Robert Borthwick had survived so many battles that everybody thought he was immortal. Unsurpassed in his mastery of cannonry, staunch and loyal, he was irreplaceable.

'How did it happen?'

'The English guns are spattering us with small metal balls. One of them hit him in the face. Our big stone balls are not very effective because they are falling short into the bog at the bottom of the hill. The English small shot cuts our men down before they even start charging.'

'That's what he feared,' said James grimly. Grimacing, he walked around for a few steps while he thought what Borthwick's death and the impotence of his artillery meant to this battle. Behind him, the mass of the Scottish army stayed stoically on the top of the hill, closing up to fill each gap that appeared when a cannonball or an archer's shaft claimed a victim. For the first time, he realized that he could lose and thousands of men could die with him. Should I retreat? he asked himself. There was still time to turn back, to order his army to march back to Coldstream and leave England to the English.

His sharp eyesight could make out individual banners among the English ranks – the flags of the Dacres, the Howards and the Bishop of Durham were lined up against him. Could he live with the shame if he let them prevail?

A sort of fatal acceptance entered into him.

No! he decided. Even if he had to die, he would fight it out, because retreating was unthinkable.

To the onlookers he looked grim, but determined and majestic as he sat on his horse surveying his enemies. Suddenly his expression lightened and he called out, 'Look, they're withdrawing. Look, they're backing away.'

Lindsay, who James had earlier wanted to hang, was staring down at the enemy too. What James said was true, Surrey's mounted knights were wheeling round and the archers drawing back.

When he saw the King preparing to chase after them, he put out a restraining hand, and said, 'Hold back, sire. Perhaps it's a ruse. Wait till you're sure what Surrey's doing. Your horse will fall on the slippy ground anyway...'

Suddenly James' composure cracked. The demon of his secret soul took him over and even his face seemed to change as he yelled, 'You again, Lindsay! Are you with us or against us? By God I'll hang you for certain when this is over! We'll chase them on foot if necessary to stop them crossing Coldstream ford before we can get at them.'

Lindsay, face set, swore an oath and spat out plainly and unafraid, 'Don't be a fool. Here you're in a strong position and he can't get at you. I'll go down if you like but you stay where you're safe, Jamie Stewart.'

'Safe! I don't want to be safe. Only cowards want safety. I'm going to kill Surrey before he gets away,' shouted the King. Before anyone could stop him, he had leapt off his horse, pulled off his boots, girded on his sword and picked up a pike.

'Out of my way!' he screamed and, with a blood-curdling yell, he swung the pike above his head and charged down the hill in his bare feet, slipping and skidding on the wet grass as he went.

First to follow him were his Highlanders, who brandished their claymores and ran in his wake screeching and howling their Gaelic battle-cry, 'Alba Gu Brath, Alba Gu Brath!' He knew that it meant 'Victory for Scotland' and shouted the words with them as he ran.

The knights who had been with him from the beginning of the enterprise looked at each other in horror but began to run down too because it was a matter of honour to follow their King. Even Lindsay ran in James' wake, though he was weeping as he did so for he knew the men who had loved and greatly admired him in his glory days were all running to their deaths, but it was unthinkable not to support the King or let him run into the middle of the enemy without backing him up and trying to protect him.

Quick to follow Lindsay was James' beloved son, the Archbishop of St Andrews, followed by Lord Maxwell, Lord Herries, the Earl of Errol and the sons and husband of the abbess of Coldstream. Errol was the first to die, spared the knowledge that eighty-seven men of his close family were also to be killed in the battle.

A mass of foot soldiers ran after them, yelling at the pitch of their lungs as they went, though many of them too knew they were committing a rash mistake and most of them were also running to a quick, cruel death. Seven thousand Englishmen stood shoulder to shoulder on the far side of the bog and watched with horror as fifteen thousand screaming Scotsmen bore down on them.

Yelling like a madman as he ran, his mind empty of everything except a lust for fighting, James Stuart headed straight for the Earl of Surrey, who sat on a heavy grey horse that had carried him through many fights.

Running alongside James, holding up the royal standard so that it fluttered bravely above his head, was his standard-bearer, Sir Adam Foreman.

At a shouted order from Surrey's son, the foot soldiers who had seemed to be in retreat turned and presented an armed front to the oncoming throng. The ruse dreamed up by the Bastard had worked. James Stewart had been enticed off the hill.

The King ran like a deer, eyes fixed on Surrey. If he thought at all, he knew he was running to his death, but he wanted to take his greatest enemy with him. The old man sat stoically watching him coming nearer and nearer, thrusting at all around him with his great pike.

An English foot soldier tried to stop him and slashed the pikestaff in half, but, throwing it down, James drew his great sword and using both hands brought it down on the head of the next man who tried to intercept him, a young knight called Richard Harbottle. The blow was so powerful that Harbottle was almost cut in half.

Surrey was now almost within James's reach … only three sword's lengths away. James fixed his eye on his quarry and swept all before him. Even when St Andrews and Foreman both fell at his side, he never faltered or looked back.

He and Surrey knew each other well and had met many times, but now the end of existence was near for one of them – but which one? Surrey was no coward but he was old and did not have the power to cut down a running man. He braced himself and stared into James' eyes. Memories of past meetings flooded into both their minds for Surrey had escorted Margaret Tudor to Scotland to marry her king and long ago he made his estimate of James' reckless character and fatal Stewart flaw.

He straightened his shoulders as he watched James raise his clenched hands with the sword's branched hilt between them. They were so close together that Surrey saw the red blood vessels that streaked the whites of his enemy's eyes. Death seemed inevitable, but just as James was about to strike him down, an arrow, fired off by a sharp-eyed

English archer, hit the King in his open, yelling mouth.

It was an amazing shot because a faction of an inch would have made a fatal difference. James would have been cut down anyway but he could have had time to kill Surrey if the arrow had glanced off his helmet. As it was, he died almost instantly, clutching at his throat, and Surrey's bodyguard, who had no idea who he was, fell on him, slashing mercilessly at his body, so mercilessly that his hands were almost severed from his arms and blood flowed from wounds that resulted from blows so strong they even pierced his armour.

The boldest and best of the Scottish nobility were cut down like ripe corn when they hit the boggy area at the bottom of the hill. Typically James had omitted to survey the ground over which he intended to fight and had no idea how much the bog would detain his men. The killing on both sides was terrible.

Impatient and uncontrollable, King James IV of Scotland ran headlong to his death, and also to the death of his kingdom. It was never again to regain the glory it knew during the early years of his reign. In a battle that lasted less than two hours, his great promise turned to dust.

Thirty-Five

From his lookout post on the top of the western ridge of Branxton Hill, Lord Home saw how the battle was progressing. Keen-eyed, he tracked Foreman carrying the bravely fluttering royal standard down the steep slope and suddenly disappearing into the mass of fighting men. It was not seen again.

That meant the King was in the middle of the melee surrounded by the enemy. There was no way he could survive. Home picked up his reins and sighed. It did not need the sight of the English soldiers pushing forward and scattering the Scottish horde to tell him the battle was lost.

Already his own army had suffered deaths. He'd seen the corpses of members of his own family, cousins, nephews and brothers, and knew there was no point sacrificing more. Home was a survivor and a realist whose cunning had brought him through many skirmishes, and he decided this was not going to be his last. The time had come to leave.

Turning in his saddle he shouted instructions to his close followers, telling them to go back to their own strongholds so that they could be defended before English raiding parties got there.

The remainder of his supporters were told to stay in position and gather up the horses when the fighting was over. He gave no orders to the mass of men that had followed him to war. As far as he was concerned, they could take their chance, either by fighting or by heading for home.

By six o'clock, when the light was fading, the Battle of Flodden was over and the fields around the village of Branxton were full of dead and dying men. As a courtesy of war, killing was suspended by the victors to give their opponents time to gather in their dead.

Men, many wounded and bloodied, wandered dazedly around, rubbing shoulders as they turned over bodies looking for friends and family. Now that the fury of killing was over and passion was spent, Englishmen and Scotsmen searched together, no longer enemies but grieving survivors.

Women camp followers who had watched the terrible killing from the sidelines ran to and fro stripping the bodies of important men of their clothes, their jewels and their arms. There were plenty of rich pickings to be found, because the cream of the Scottish nobility was cut down that day. Sometimes a woman turned over a well-clad body and found that life was still in it. Indifferent to moans and pleas for help, she took what she wanted and left the man to die naked and unattended.

There were male body robbers too, among them Sam Lee, who had managed to save his own skin during the fighting though his brothers were all dead. Ironically it was Sam who came upon the blood-smeared body of the King, who lay in a heap of corpses that included his son and Adam Foreman.

Delighted at his good fortune in finding the richest bodies on the field, Sam set about stripping them, taking off their rings and necklets first before finally pulling the slashed red and gold surcoat off James. Remembering his time as the fake King, he could not resist putting it on and that was his fatal mistake, for as he stood up a dying English soldier who was staggering past saw the coat, recognized it and thinking that the King of Scotland had survived, thrust his sword through Sam's throat as his last gesture of despair.

Sam fell to his knees and toppled onto the corpse of the Archbishop of St Andrews. A few moments later, before the last breath left his body, a Romany woman came upon him, and cried out in delight when she discovered the stolen jewels and golden chain on him, pulling them out of his pocket and off his neck, before tying them up in her apron and running away with them. She made her fortune that day.

Robert Fletcher and the men of Selkirk fought valiantly till they found themselves cut off by Dacre's men, who succeeded in wresting the Selkirk standard away from Robert. This was regarded as a terrible loss by the Fletchers, who could not contemplate returning home without it. Massing together, they charged into the middle of a party of men from Macclesfield who were gathered round their town's flag, and after hard hand-to-hand fighting wrested that flag away as a trophy of war.

They had an enemy flag, but of all of them only Robert and a man he knew to be a smallholder and dairyman from outside Selkirk were the survivors of the skirmish. Everyone else was dead.

The two survivors stared bleakly at each other. They had only been slight acquaintances before riding off to war but now they had very much in common.

'Are you hurt?' Robert asked.

'Aye. My arm was cut when I was grabbing for the flag.'

'Let's see.'

They examined the man's wound and Robert tore up a corpse's shirt to make a bandage, but he could see that the wound was deep and still bleeding. He himself was in pain from a spear thrust to his thigh, but he deliberately tried to ignore this suffering for he had only one thought in his mind.

'We've got to get back to Selkirk,' he said grimly.

'Aye, and what terrible news we're going to bring them! Seventy-eight men dead,' said the dairyman.

'But they have to know. And we're the only ones that can tell them. We've got to head for home.'

One of the Home henchmen was passing and Robert called out to him, 'What's going on?'

The man came over and looked mournfully at them and their bloodstained clothes. 'You're both in a bad way. My lord's retreated and we've to gather up the horses. Where are you from?'

'Selkirk.'

'And you're the only ones left?'

'Aye.'

'At least there's two of you. I'm from Gordon myself. All the men from Hawick are dead, and it's the same for Galashiels.'

Robert stared bleakly at this bringer of bad news, who was intimidated by his hopeless eyes, and went on, 'I'm going over the hill to make sure that our horses arenae all stolen. I'll find two for you. Just stay here till I come back.'

'And will you? Why should we trust

Home's man when Home himself has run away?'

'I'll come back. I promise.'

He was as good as his word and soon returned with two good horses, both saddled and bridled. 'Get out of here,' he told them, 'and head for Yetholm. It's a long way round but it'll be safer than going by Coldstream. When they gather themselves together again, the English will be picking us off at the Tweed crossing. That's what Home was afraid of...'

Alarmed by his urgency, the Selkirk men heaved themselves into their saddles and rode off at once. Mindful of the warning about English soldiers, they rolled up the Macclesfield flag and tied it behind the dairyman's saddle. It seemed they had a very long road to ride before they saw Selkirk again.

In the confusion when the pikemen were regrouping on the hill after Home withdrew, Peter lost Thomas. Searching around for him in a panic, he was swept along in a rush of Highlanders who were following the King into the bog. Peter fell when he ran into the edge of the quagmire and lay helpless while running men used his back as a bridge. The King was killed not more than fifty yards away from him but he saw none of that because he lay supine like a corpse and that saved him.

On hands and knees he eventually crawled out, caked with mud and blood, because, though he himself was unharmed, many men had been slaughtered beside him. He sat up and saw he was in a field of corpses. Was Thomas among them, he wondered.

Trying to control his shaking body, he squatted on the ground and tried to remember where he'd last seen his brother. Thomas would not be likely to take part in any charge. In fact he'd probably run in the opposite direction.

Painfully, on hands and knees because the slope was so greasy and torn up, Peter made his way back up to the top of the hill, where looters were already helping themselves to the contents of the royal tent. He stopped a wild-looking woman, and said to her, 'I'm looking for my brother...'

'You'll have a hard search,' she said shortly.

'But he's not a real soldier. He's a bit simple. Have you seen him?'

She was kindly in spite of her appearance. 'I've seen a daftie. He was running that way,' and she pointed south to where the baggage wagons were drawn up. Already English soldiers had closed in on them and were preparing to haul them away, but not before they helped themselves to ale from the kegs that were piled on one of them. Of course, thought Peter, Tom would run back to where he'd last seen Lucy.

He went slowly down towards the wagons trying not to attract the attention of the Englishmen. The body of one of the old men who had looked after Lucy was lying blood-soaked under a cart but there was no sign of the other and no sign of Tom. Despondently Peter withdrew and was walking aimlessly back to the western camp when he saw the other old carter sitting among a group of women – and, Deo gratias, Thomas was with him.

'Thank God! I thought I'd lost you,' he cried, running towards his brother.

Thomas looked up and showed a tear-stained face. 'The Englishmen killed Old Tom because he wouldn't give them ale but me and Willie ran away,' he said.

Peter hunkered down beside them and said gently, 'It's all right if you're safe. We'll go home now, I think.'

'But I've not seen the real King yet.'

'That doesn't matter. You're not hurt, are you?'

A stricken Willie spoke up. 'He's fine. He came running up looking for his sister but we sent her away yesterday. She should be home by now.'

'I want to see the King,' said Thomas stubbornly.

'Get up and I'll take you to see him,' said Peter soothingly, but then looked at Willie and asked, 'What's the best thing to do?'

'Head for Coldstream. People say the ford's still open and the nuns'll help you. Try to catch a pair of loose horses. There's plenty of them running aboot. It's all over, lad. Get oot as fast as you can.'

'What about you?' asked Peter.

'I'll stay here with the women. Home's run away, my old freend is dead and I've naething to gang back to Kelsae for. It's over for me too.'

Holding Thomas's hand, Peter led him back down the hill to where so many bodies lay. The first thing that struck him was the silence. After the blood-curdling howls and screams of fighting that had rung out only half an hour before, a deadly stillness hung over the battlefield. Dead-eyed men wandered about and bodies lay at grotesque angles among the reeds of the bog. Already the water in the burn that ran at the foot of the hill had taken on the reddish tinge of blood. It would flow red for three days to come.

Parties of English soldiers had already started on the task of collecting their dead, and people came out of hiding in Branxton village to help with the horrific task. When an old man saw the brothers heading for the road to Coldstream, he shouted, 'Stay, we need help. All those bodies have to be taken off the field before the crows and foxes get them.'

Peter paused and pulled Tom back. 'Come on, we should help,' he said. He felt it was the least he could do, for after all he and his brother had survived and it would be insensitive to ignore the duty of giving even a cursory burial to the others who did not.

Though Thomas was still suffering from his cut arm, they were both strong and they found themselves heaving naked dead men onto their shoulders like sacks of meal in their father's mill and carrying them to the church, where they heaped them in the porch, hoping that friends would come to identify them and give them a burial.

When they were laying a blond-haired Englishman alongside a red-haired Highlander, Thomas suddenly gave a cry and pointed at another body lying on the porch floor.

'Peter, look, it's Sam Lee,' he called to his brother who ran over.

'But that the King's surcoat he's wearing,' said a Branxton man, who was working with them.

'It's no' the King. It's Sam Lee,' persisted Thomas, staring into the distorted face.

'Who was he?' asked the stranger.

'A horse thief who comes from near our home. He probably stole the surcoat,' said Peter shortly. He trusted Thomas because he'd picked out Sam every time he masqueraded as the King.

'You're probably right. If it is the King he'd be wearing armour and not just a torn surcoat over an old jerkin that isn't worth stealing. Leave him here with the others,' said the Branxton man.

Their work went on even after darkness fell and by that time the church porch was full and bodies were laid out in the churchyard among the graves. After work stopped for the night, Peter and Thomas, exhausted and hungry, lay down to sleep in an empty barn by the church and a sympathetic local woman, who'd seen how hard they'd worked, gave them a share of the supper she'd made for her own family. It was a kind gift for food was scarce, especially for the losers of the battle.

Though Thomas complained that his injured arm was hurting, they slept like dead men. When Peter woke it was still dark and he had trouble remembering where he was and everything that had happened during the previous terrible day. Suddenly realization dawned and he looked across at his brother, who was groaning with the pain of his arm. He must get Thomas home to the tender care of their mother as soon as possible. She was skilled with cures.

But first he wanted to try to find Sandy, or if not Sandy alive, at least his body. Thank God the kind old men had made Lucy run for home. And he had to find horses because

Thomas did not look capable of walking any distance.

There were loose horses scattered far and wide but people would start rounding them up as soon as dawn broke.

He gently shook his brother by the shoulder and said, 'Get up, lad. We have to find horses and we've got to look for Sandy.'

They emerged into a pale grey dawn but even so early there were already people about. To Peter's surprise, the first he saw was a group of nuns led by a tall black-clad woman with a haggard face. At the end of their line was a ragged little figure carrying a big basket.

Thomas recognized her first. 'It's Lucy!' he cried and ran towards her.

She turned, dropped the basket and threw her arms round him, sobbing as she said, 'It's you, it's really you. I was afraid that you'd be killed. Where's Peter?'

'I'm here,' said a voice behind her and she whipped round to hug him too. 'Oh, thank God you're both safe. This is so awful. Look at all those poor dead men. The abbess brought us over to see if we could help more of the wounded but most of them have run away, or been taken home by their friends. It's the dead we have to look after now and try to find out who they were.'

'We found Sam Lee's body and brought it into the church last night and I've recognized some others. But I'm still looking for Sandy. Have you seen him?' said Peter.

'Yes, I have. He's safe too. I saw him a little while ago. He's helping to dig a burial pit at the other side of the village. The bodies that aren't claimed are to be thrown in and covered up ... It's terrible. There's so many of them. The abbess says people will only know who is lost when they don't return home again.'

Thirty-Six

When Surrey and his son withdrew victorious from the field, they held council with the other commanders in their tents not far from Ford. Their first melancholy task was to find out who was dead, and, as they suspected, though some several hundred Englishmen were killed, their losses were nothing like as cataclysmic as those of the Scots. At least fifteen thousand of them lay dead on Flodden field.

'Jamie Stewart is gone,' said old Surrey, 'I saw him killed.'

'We must get hold of his body. Queen Catherine sent us a message to find it because she wants to send his head to France

285

so Henry will know that the Scots are truly vanquished,' said Howard.

Surrey father grimaced. It was not his way to desecrate the corpses of dead enemies. 'The Queen is very Spanish, very savage,' he said and no one contradicted him.

'We must send her the body, though,' his son persisted.

'That will be done. The abbess of Coldstream is in Branxton now looking for it. She knows Jamie well and has promised that she will hand him over to me. Then we can send the body south. What the Queen does with it is her affair,' said Surrey with a sigh. He was deathly tired and anxious for this expedition to end. Though some of his advisers urged following the fleeing Scottish army back over the Border, he refused.

'What's the point?' he asked. 'What's left of them are broken and powerless. Their King and all their best men are dead. It would not be right to sack a nation that is already on its knees. They will not oppose Henry for the rest of his life. Moreover our own army is exhausted, short of provisions and ravaged with plague.'

He was well aware that he was not at the head of a conquering army any more. The consequences of this battle would be passed onto lesser lords like Dacre, and ordinary people in Scottish cottages, farmhouses and hovels would be harried by raiding from

286

Northumbria later.

The thought of raiding lords made him look around at the men beside him and ask, 'Where's Bastard Heron? We mustn't forget it was he who made this victory possible for us.'

'Not entirely,' demurred Stanley.

'He brought our men through Pallinsburn bog. That gave us the advantage,' said Surrey. 'Where is he?'

'*Dead*,' said Dacre.

Everyone looked at him, for they were well aware of the hatred that existed between Dacre and the Herons.

'How did he die?' asked Surrey.

'He was facing up to Home, he was about to kill him when someone stabbed him in the back. I'd have done it if I could but it wasn't me. It was some other enemy of his who was fighting on our side. He hated Heron more than he hated the Scotsman.'

'Someone? It had to be done from the back because he would have cut down anyone who tried to take him from the front.' Surrey's voice was caustic. He was not convinced by Dacre's protestations of innocence.

'He was a brave and resourceful man,' agreed Howard.

'But wicked,' said Constable, who was on Dacre's side.

'Wicked or not, I made promises to him and they must be carried out. No one, and especially not you, Dacre, must touch any of the Herons' possessions till his brother gets back from Fast Castle. I'll make sure he is released soon,' was Surrey's final word.

Lady Heron waited in the only unburned tower of her stronghold for the return of her men. She raised her arms in glee when news was brought to her that James Stewart and his son were dead, but her mood quickly changed when that news was followed by information that the Bastard had been cut down. She had never been sure which of the Heron brothers she loved best.

'My lord and your father will be home soon,' she told her children when she stopped crying.

'How can you be sure?' asked her daughter.

'Because the Scots lord of Fast Castle was killed yesterday and most of his followers as well. I've sent a rider north with money to pay the gateman to let your father out. He will be freed very soon,' she said and she was right.

Throughout the day, with their skirts kirtled up like bondagers and heavy boots on their feet, the nuns of Coldstream went from body to body in Branxton churchyard looking for signs of life or some evidence of identity.

It was a hard task because the body robbers had been busy and most of the corpses were naked, at least those of rich men were. Only the poorest had been dressed in nothing worth stealing.

Throughout the day the nuns were joined in their task by stunned survivors turning over lacerated bodies and studying faces in search of a father, a brother or a son. Many of them found the people they were seeking and groaned in grief at the discovery.

Sometimes they loaded the dead man over the pommel of a horse's saddle and headed for home so that the casualty could be buried in his home ground, others walked away with tears in their eyes, leaving the body to be thrown into one of the vast pits that were being dug in the fields around the village.

Abbess Isabella did not shirk even the most gruesome tasks and joined her nuns in searching for signs of life among ivory white corpses. After a few hours, she surprised the women around her by drawing back with a gasp when she found her own husband.

He was lying in a pile of bodies, his eyes white, open and staring up at her as if he could see into her soul. Fear clutched at her heart, and fear was not an emotion that she felt very often.

'Wedderburn,' she whispered, half expecting to hear him answer, but he kept on sightlessly staring and there was a film of death over his eyeballs.

The young girl Lucy was passing by and the abbess turned to say, 'Help me drag this man into the church.'

Lucy took an arm and pulled while the abbess pulled on the other. When they laid him down in the chancel, Isabella crossed herself and sprinkled some of the holy water from a stoup near the door over his face.

Wondering why this particular corpse, a tall grey-haired man with lacerations on his arms and body, was receiving such special attention, Lucy whispered, 'Who is he?'

'My husband,' said the abbess. Her mouth was tight and her eyes cold and tearless. She wondered if she should tell this girl that she loved him once when they were both young, that she had borne him seven sons and had suffered his infidelities with dignity before she left him to take up the religious life.

The girl stared at her in incomprehension, wondering how she could conduct herself with such apparent indifference, but she had recovered herself by now and gestured with a brisk nod of the head towards the door. 'There's more work to be done,' she ordered.

Ironically, that after a period of drear weather and continual rain, the 10th of September dawned bright and clear, a perfect autumn day. The hedges round the churchyard were bright with rosehips that glowed scarlet like drops of blood, and, as Lucy breathed in, she tasted frost in the air. I want to go home, oh how I want to be safe at home, she thought.

The death and gore that surrounded her were so appalling that it seemed impossible that both her brothers had survived. When she turned her head, she could see them in the distance dragging bodies to the burial pits. She too had work to do before she could go home.

The tall abbess was striding off in front of her and she followed at a half run, so she was within hearing distance when a tall young man about the same age as Peter came running up and stood in the nun's way.

'God damn you, mother. I hope you rot in Hell,' he cried in a terrible voice.

The abbess put out a hand to touch him but he brushed it roughly away. 'If you hadn't sent him back, he'd still be alive. He told me what you said to him. You called him a coward and he was never that!'

'I told him it was his duty to fight for his King,' she said bleakly, because they both knew who they were talking about.

'Duty! You're very strong on duty. Well, he's dead now and so are my other brothers and my father. I hope you're satisfied that we have made a big enough blood sacrifice.'

'Your father's lying inside the church,' she told him. Only the trembling of her lips showed that she was fighting with intense emotion but her son did not care.

'I blame you. If you had allowed my brother to go home as our father wanted, I would have one brother left and our lands would be safe. The English are probably sacking it now,' he spat.

'I loved him too,' she said.

'You've never loved anyone except your precious God. You've always preferred praying instead of listening to any of us. I think you are a monster without a heart.'

'Oh, I have a heart and it is aching today. Go and get your father's corpse and take him home. Where are your brothers' bodies?'

'Thrown into the burial pit over there ... Go and say your prayers over them too if you think it will help them.' Tears began running down his face and Lucy wondered how the abbess could not throw her arms round him, but she seemed stern-faced, standing apart from him with her hands tucked inside the cuffs of her long sleeves. Inside, however, she was in terrible turmoil.

When she looked round and saw Lucy watching, she collected herself and said loudly, 'Here's more work to be done, don't stand there gawking.'

As she walked beside the hurrying girl, Isabella lectured herself. 'I must not think about this ... I have work to do ... I must try to find the body of the King...' It would be weak to weep, to slump down and mourn.

She was a noblewoman and noblewomen did not show weakness. Above all she was a Scottish noblewoman from a family with a long tradition of service to the crown. No matter what frailties and faults Jamie Stewart may have had, he was the anointed King and her duty was to him.

Playing her usual diplomatic game, she had agreed to pass the body on to Surrey if she found it, but secretly had no intention of doing so. It was imperative to find his body before anyone else did so it could be given a decent burial and she must prevent the English from getting their hands on it because she knew what indignities victors inflicted on the bodies of their enemies. *That must not happen to Scotland's king.*

Turning to the girl by her side, she asked, 'Have you ever seen King James?'

'Only from a distance, but my brothers over there have seen him,' was the answer.

'Where are they exactly?'

'Just over there, taking bodies to be buried.'

'Fetch them. I need their help.'

When Lucy brought Peter and Thomas to the abbess, she said, 'Your sister tells me you would recognize the King's body.'

Peter looked at the nun's grim face and said slowly, 'That depends on how badly he was injured...' He had seen many bodies that were so lacerated they were almost unrecognizable as men, far less as individuals.

'All I need is for you to sort out men who might be him and show them to me because I know him well. I've known him since he was a boy.'

'I know him too,' said the second boy and for the first time she noticed that he was a simpleton. She recognized the signs only too well because her own youngest son, one of the two left at home, was a simpleton too.

'Then you'll be able to help your brother search for him,' she said in an almost kindly tone that surprised Lucy.

It was a gruesome task, and they all took part in it, even the abbess. She knew the King's body had been brought into the churchyard and she would not allow anyone to remove a body without examining it first. Excitedly she ran over when one of a burial party turned over a tall corpse and called out, 'I think this is the King!'

The face and neck were badly mutilated, but the long dark hair remained, and so did the stubbly reddish beard.

'Wasn't his beard very long?' she asked doubtfully.

A nobleman, one of the Ramsays who was searching for his son, came over and looked. 'He had it cut off before the fighting started. It was tangling in his helmet straps. I saw him doing it.'

'It does look like him,' everyone agreed and started pulling the body out of the heap, but then Thomas looked closely at the face and said, 'That's no' the King, that's Sam Lee.'

Peter believed him. 'He's always right,' he told the abbess.

She bent down again and pulled at the tatters that clung around the body. 'I'm checking. He always wore an iron penitential chain round his waist and even if he's been robbed that wouldn't have been worth stealing,' she said. When she saw there was no chain on the body, she stepped back disappointed.

'It's Sam Lee, the horse thief,' insisted Thomas again.

Lucy was looking over another pile of corpses in the church doorway. 'But there's one with a chain round its waist,' she said, pointing.

The abbess ran across, grimaced at the severity of the wounds on the body and cried, 'I think it is him. Clever girl!' With a reverence that she had not shown before she knelt beside it and pulled at the iron chain, examining it for a lock or clasp. When she found the improvised tie, she said with relief, 'Thank God I can get it off without sending for a blacksmith.'

Then an idea struck her.

'Get the one you say is Sam Lee and bring it into the chancel,' she ordered Peter and when the chain was gently pulled from the corpse, she handed it to Lucy with another order. 'Take that to the boys and tell them to put it on the horse thief's body.'

Lucy she did as she was told and Peter did the same because he had seen enough of the abbess to realize she knew what she was doing,

When Lucy returned to the porch she found the abbess and another nun wrapping James up in a winding cloth.

'He must be taken to a place of safety. The English must not get their hands on him,' said Isabella grimly.

The nun nodded in agreement. 'They'd make a spectacle of him. An English soldier told me that their Queen wants to send his head to her husband in France.'

'She can send the horse thief's head. It won't make any difference to him,' said the abbess shortly. 'He can't be buried here. Surrey's men are looking for him. I could send him to Yetholm. Bodies have gone there for burial already, but they might be watching there too. He should go to a place of peace and dignity...'

She turned to Lucy. 'Your brothers must take the King to a place of safety where he can be buried in secret. They can get away with it because anyone they meet will think they're just another pair of survivors taking a brother home.'

Lucy looked down at the ravaged body and

said quietly, 'I know where to bury him. Dryburgh Abbey near my home is beautiful and secluded. My brothers will take him there.'

The abbess clasped her hands. 'The perfect place! I know the abbot there. He will keep his counsel. Take my king to Dryburgh.'

Placing a hand on the linen-wrapped head of the corpse, she said softly, 'Goodbye, James. You had great promise and died like a hero, but a mistaken one.'

Striding out of the church, she mounted her mare and rode back to Coldstream, from where she sent a secret messenger to Dryburgh and another more openly to Surrey's camp.

'Tell the Earl that I have identified the body of the King and will give it into his custody,' she told the second messenger.

As usual she was placating potential enemies but her own feelings were more deeply engaged than ever before.

Thirty-Seven

In early dawn, a foam-flecked horse galloped into the vast courtyard in front of Holyrood Palace. Anxious guards came running out to help an exhausted man out of the saddle and hear what he had to say.

'It's over. They fought. He's dead. They're all dead,' the rider gasped and sank to his knees on the cobbles.

An old man helped him up. 'Not Jamie? Not the King? Not my ain son, Robbie Mackay?' he asked.

'The King and a' the grand lords and your lad too. Douglas, Mar, Huntly, Gordon, Sinclair, Elphinstone, Lennox – all of them are dead.' He gagged and vomited as he gasped more names out.

The guards stared at each other unable to believe such a scale of horror. 'Spread the news,' gasped the messenger and sank to his knees again

The Queen was abruptly roused by a white-faced woman. 'Wake up, my lady,' she said, shaking the plump shoulder.

Almost before her eyes were open, Margaret asked, 'Is he dead?'

They knew who she meant and answered with one word. 'Yes.'

As if she was prodded by a spear, the Queen jumped out of bed, issuing orders before her feet touched the ground. She'd spent most of the night working out, with Tudor calculation, what to do if the worst happened and had only fallen asleep a short time before the awaited news of the battle arrived.

'Fetch my son. My boxes are packed. Get Douglas. Get the horses.'

Her woman was surprised by this unusual spurt of energy and decision because Margaret had spent the last few days in a strange lethargy.

'Where will you go, madam?' they asked.

'Home. I'm going home.'

'To Linlithgow?'

'Don't be stupid. I'm going to England. My brother will look after me. My son and I will be safer with him than with the warring lords here.'

'But the man who brought the news said there's no great lords left. They're all dead. The burgesses of Edinburgh have started building a great wall round the city to keep the English out. You'll be safe here.'

'No, I won't. I'm an Englishwoman, re-member. There's bound to be enough great lords left to make trouble for my son and me.' Like other people who had not been at Flodden, Margaret was having trouble comprehending the scale of the disaster.

It was only after the Queen's long retinue clattered out of the palace courtyard that those left behind realized she had not shed a single tear.

Young Douglas accompanied her for the first stretch of the journey but by the time they arrived in Haddington, he told her, 'I can't go with you into England. All my brothers are dead and my father's spirit is broken. I'm riding back to meet him.'

She did not seem to care very much. All she was thinking about was getting herself and the young heir out of Scotland. 'I'll go to Fast Castle and try to find another escort there,' she said.

The guide she got was Lord Heron, who the frightened guards released, and were glad to see the back of. He escorted her to Berwick on Tweed.

When the immense walls of the old town and its huge castle reared up in front of her party, she turned in her litter, for she could not ride a horse for fear of losing the baby in her womb, and cried out in relief, 'Send a messenger into the town to tell them Margaret Tudor and her son have arrived and are seeking sanctuary.'

The reply was not what she expected. 'The

burgesses of Berwick send their compliments to Margaret Tudor and her son but regret they cannot allow them to enter Berwick.'

She went scarlet with fury. 'Why not?' she asked the dignified man who brought this unwelcome news.

'The town fears for its security if it receives Scotland's runaway queen and her son who is now the King of that country.'

Like people in Edinburgh, even the burghers of Berwick did not realize how badly Scotland had been emasculated. They did not realize there were not enough great lords left to go chasing after their next king. In spite of Margaret's fury, the town gates were closed to her.

Where to go? She lay back in the litter and allowed herself to shed a first tear. A messenger must be sent to her brother's wife, with whom she had never enjoyed good relations, asking for safe conduct to enter England. But where would she be safe till the permission arrived?

Coldstream! She had always been generous in her donations to the abbey there. The abbess, with whom she often corresponded, would take her in.

Frantic and weeping, she directed her retinue to turn round and head west up the Tweed. They travelled in darkness, so the scenes of carnage and straggles of shocked survivors from both sides that they passed on the way were hidden from her.

Abbess Isabella hid her dismay when she saw the royal retinue turning in the abbey gate. Though she was always cordial whenever they met or corresponded, she did not like the Queen, who she considered trivial and fickle, for, since no gossip of the court escaped her, she knew about the ongoing flirtation with young Douglas.

But, as usual, she weighed up the chances of benefits for the abbey from giving shelter to the Queen, who was also Henry Tudor's sister, and more importantly to her son, the new King of Scotland.

'Welcome to my humble abbey,' she said smoothly when the royal retinue rode in.

Though she passed on much news to her royal visitor, she did not admit seeing the King's corpse and did not say that two days before Margaret's arrival at Coldstream, the body of her husband had been secretly removed from any danger of being treated shamefully by the English victors.

The body of Sam Lee was delivered to Surrey, but without the chain the abbess had so carefully placed around his waist. The man she put in charge of handing it over, secretly unwrapped the corpse on the way to see if there was anything worth stealing on it, for he had heard stories about James always wearing a chain as a penance. To his delight he found a chain was still on him but apparently broken, so he slipped it off and put it in the leather pouch he wore at his waist for examining later.

When he got the chance to look at it properly he found it was not made of precious metal as he had hoped, but only of iron and was valueless.

'You'd think there would be something more valuable than an old harness chain on a king,' he angrily told his son who sat with him on the cart carrying the body.

While he was grumbling about the poverty of his booty, Surrey and those of his officers who knew the Scottish king were standing around the unwrapped corpse and staring at it critically.

'It certainly looks like him, but where's the chain he always wore?' asked Howard.

'The scavengers will have it, just as they have taken all his fine rings as well,' said Somerset dismissively, lifting a curling lock of black hair and dropping it again.

'Perhaps we should call in Lady Heron to identify some other parts of him,' said a member of Howard's retinue with a laugh.

Surrey frowned. 'This is the body of a king, remember. I don't approve of jeering at a dead man, especially a dead king. I knew him in life and remember him well, but his face is now so disfigured that I can't be certain.'

'The hair's his, anyway. I remember my wife admiring it ten years ago when we met him at his meeting with the Tudor wench,' said Dacre.

'Yes, it's his hair, and what remains of the beard looks red ... Send the body to the embalmers and tell them to carry it to Newcastle for the journey south. I'll write to Queen Catherine and ask her to treat it with dignity,' said Surrey in a weary voice.

'It's a trophy of war,' his son reminded him, but he only sighed again for there was no glory in it as far as he was concerned.

Thirty-Eight

At Yetholm, the Selkirk dairyman suddenly fell from his horse.

An old man in a blacksmith's apron stepped forward and picked him up. He looked at Fletcher sitting like a ramrod on his horse and said, 'He's dead.'

'Will you bury him?'

'Aye.'

'Then give me the bundle from behind his saddle. I've got to take it home.'

The rolled-up Macclesfield flag was passed up to him and he laid it across his pommel.

With pity evident on his face, the black-smith asked, 'Where is your home? Where are you heading?'

'Selkirk.' Speaking was an effort for Fletch-er and he felt as if his life was ebbing away with the blood that seeped from his wound and stained his breeches.

'That's a long ride.'

'Is it?' The man on the horse seemed barely aware of what he was saying.

'You're wounded. Get down and rest. You can have food with us.'

A woman behind the blacksmith said, 'Yes, we have food hidden away and we'll be happy to share it with you. You can sleep here too.'

Fletcher shook his head. 'No. I must go home. They don't know what's happened yet...'

'They'll hear soon enough,' said the old man and shook his head.

In spite of their concerned pleading, Fletcher stuck his heels in the horse's flanks and headed west. 'What about your other horse?' the blacksmith called behind him.

'Keep it!'

The ride home seemed endless, across vast empty moors, following sheep tracks over the foothills of the Cheviots. His horse plod-ded on, and sometimes he fell asleep in the saddle, waking up to find the reins loose on the horse's neck as it quietly ate grass or drank from a stream. He had no idea how long he slept; he had no idea how many days he'd been on the road. He felt disembodied, as if he was floating above himself.

With detached interest he looked at the spreading bloodstains on his clothes and wondered how long it would take for his entire blood supply to seep away.

'I must get home. I must get back to Selkirk,' he kept muttering.

Every time he rode through a village, people came out of their cottages and stood staring solemn-faced while the church bells tolled out a dirge. On the third day, his horse walked slowly through the village of Midlem. Again people came running out to watch him, and call out questions. 'Is it true the King's dead? How many men got away? Have you seen our blacksmith Tom Syme, a big man with bright red hair?'

He was too exhausted to answer, only able to shake his head and wave a dismissive hand in answer to their questions. 'Selkirk, Selkirk,' he kept muttering, determined to see his home town and his family again.

A man who heard this ran alongside and offered him a fresh horse because the one that had carried him so far was walking slowly with its head hanging down, but he waved the offer away. Nothing would get him out of the saddle, so the concerned man got on the fresh horse and galloped off to warn Selkirk that one of the townsmen was on his way.

It was evening when Robert Fletcher looked down from a hilltop and saw smoke rising from his town's chimneys into the still September air.

'Home!' He sat up straighter in the saddle and summoned the last of his strength.

'Home!' he told the horse and shook the reins but it had nothing left to give. Very slowly they staggered down the hill to the west port, where a crowd of frightened-looking people waited for him.

'Who is it?' they asked each other as the ragged rider rode in.

'Rob Fletcher, it's Rob Fletcher,' the word ran round, fetching all the Fletcher wives out of their houses, running to the barred gate with tears pouring from their eyes.

Men opened the town gate and crowded round him, trying to help him off the horse, but he pushed them away with the last of his strength. 'The town cross. I must get to the town cross,' he muttered and the crowd parted to form a pathway through which he rode.

The stone town cross, surmounted by a lion rampant, rose from the middle of the crowded square. All the doors in the houses round it were open and men, women and children stood staring at Fletcher as he dismounted. Staggering he pulled the Macclesfield flag off his saddle and unfurled it so they all could see.

'I lost the town flag but I brought this back in its place. I lost my brothers. Oh, alas, Selkirk has lost all its men,' he called out and sank to his knees, to be caught in the arms of his weeping brother Edward, who held his head as he died.

Mounted on three sturdy horses provided by the abbess, Lucy, Peter and Thomas, who was in growing pain from his cut arm and seemed to be running a fever but refused to stay and be nursed by the concerned nuns, set out for home on a sunny autumn morning.

Peter was leading a fourth horse, a dead English knight's stallion that had been stabbed in the shoulder by a Scottish pikeman. The wound was not deep but it was open and the horse was terrified and would not carry a rider, so it was chosen by the abbess to be the bearer of the body of the King. She reckoned that when it recovered, as it would, the young people would have a good horse as a reward for their trouble.

Wrapped in dirty sacking, because it was to be explained away as the body of their poor neighbour, the corpse lay across the war horse's back and though it tried to buck its burden off, it was well tied down and stayed in place.

They travelled slowly along the northern bank of the Tweed, meeting a few other shocked survivors on their way. Again, in every village they rode through, the church bells pealed out mournfully.

When they reached Birgham, they came upon a man walking alone and Lucy cried out in delighted surprise. 'Sandy! Thank God you're safe.'

Sandy was always cheerful, even in terrible circumstances, and he looked up at her with a broad grin on his face. 'I'm hard tae kill and I stayed alive to marry you,' he told her.

She blushed but Sandy didn't notice. 'Thon's grand-looking animals you have there. Did you steal them?' he said, because he was a skilled rider and a connoisseur of horses.

'The abbess of Coldstream gave them to us,' said Thomas, ignoring Peter's warning look.

'That was lucky. She's said to be a hard woman, that abbess. What's that?' he asked, pointing at the wrapped body on the fourth horse.

'It's Sam Lee,' said Peter, but Thomas chipped in, 'It isnae. Ye ken fine it's the King.'

That took the smile off Sandy's face. 'The King?' he repeated in a voice of disbelief.

'Dinna tell onybody,' warned Thomas.

Peter looked at his sister and said in a despairing voice, 'We'll have to stop him saying that.'

She turned in the saddle and looked at her youngest brother. 'You mustn't tell anybody about the King because if the English get him they'll cut him in pieces and stick the bits on London Bridge for people to throw rubbish at.' That was what the abbess had told her.

Thomas was as shocked as she had been. 'Oh, they cannae dae that. We'll hide him in the mill.'

'That's right, so you mustn't tell folk the body's not Sam Lee.'

'So they can cut Sam up instead,' agreed Thomas happily.

After that, of course, they had to let Sandy in on the secret, and he stood staring at the body on the horse's back with a look of awe on his face.

'That's the King. King James,' he said slowly. Then he turned to Lucy and asked cheekily, 'Do you think he'd mind if I share his horse? I'm tired of walking.'

'It's a wild horse. It wouldn't let anybody on its back. That's why we got it,' she told him.

'It'll let me,' said Sandy confidently and walked over to pull down the horse's head, and gently fondle its ears while he muttered softly and breathed into its nostrils. It stood quietly listening to him, fine skin twitching. After a few minutes, he jumped gently onto its back, taking care not to brush against its wound, and again it accepted him.

'Let's go home,' he said, laying one hand on the corpse of the King.

'We have to go to Dryburgh first. The abbess said she'd send a message to the abbot and he'll have a grave ready for the King,' Lucy told him.

'We have to deliver him before we go home because if mother finds out who he is she'll spread the news to everybody round about,' Peter added.

'If anyone sees us we'll say it's Sam Lee,' said Lucy.

As the countryside around them grew more familiar, a strange feeling of solemnity seized them all. Even Sandy stopped joking. All of them were desperate to see their homes again, and Thomas whimpered, 'I want to see my mother. I want to go home.'

But Peter was determined. 'We're going to Dryburgh first. Then we'll go home afterwards. Look, it's not far now,' he said, pointing down into the Tweed valley to where the tower and arches of the abbey were peeping above the trees on the north side of the river.

'The river doesn't look too full. We should try to cross at the abbey ford,' said Sandy, urging his horse towards the muddy track that led to the river edge. Facing it from the opposite bank was a gatehouse that looked far more homely and welcoming than the gateway of Coldstream abbey. A man armed with a billhook was guarding it and when he saw them, he waved and yelled, 'The abbot's been waiting for you. It's safe to cross. Come on.'

A group of solemn-faced monks waited for them in the green enclosure beside the cloisters as Sandy and Peter carried in their precious burden and laid it down on the paved walkway in the shadow under the arches. It seemed very long as it lay there.

The abbot looked down at it asked, 'Are you sure it's the King?'

'The abbess said it was. You can look too if you like but he's very badly injured,' Peter told him.

'We'll look,' said the abbot, and gestured to his monks to carry the body into their infirmary.

The young people sat down in the shade and a lay brother brought them a jug of ale with bread and cheese, which was more than welcome for they'd eaten little on their journey. On its way to be eliminated, the Scottish army had emptied the lower Tweed valley of food.

They were leaning back sated when the abbot reappeared. 'Though he seems to have been killed by an arrow through his mouth,

I think it is James. I saw him several times but then he was in his glory. We'll bury him now. Do you want to attend the ceremony?'

An aged monk leaned towards him and pointed at Lucy as he said, 'That's a lassie. You can't let a woman into the sanctuary.'

'Brother Dominick, I think we can make an exception and allow this young woman in. You can pretend she's a boy if you like because she's dressed as one, isn't she? Without her help we would not have a body to bury,' said the abbot firmly and the old man stepped back, disapproving but unable to object.

The King's body, wrapped in a fine piece of embroidered cloth, was lowered into a grave excavated in the floor beside the abbey altar. Censers were swung, the air was full of the smell of incense, and the high clear voices of the monks' choir soared into the evening sky as the abbot delivered the burial service and commended the soul of King James IV to his maker.

The four young people, who had carried the vainglorious, magnificent man to his secret resting place, wept when sanctified earth was piled over him.

They rode home with their heads drooping and a terrible tiredness engulfing them.

When Peter, Thomas and Lucy clattered into the mill yard, they were greeted by their weeping parents and a white-faced Ishbel, who had lost her baby shortly after Sam Lee rode away. Lucy knew from her sister's face that she wanted to know what had happened to him, for the word had got back about the terrible slaughter.

'He's dead,' she whispered, 'I saw his body.'

Ishbel wept and threw her arms around her sister.

Lucy's father was so relieved to have her safely back that he never uttered a word of reproof about her rashness in taking off after the army. She stayed happily at home for two years before she married Sandy and went to live at his farm, which was now locally known as Sorrowlessfield because all three sons of the place returned safely and their farm was the only one in the district that did not lose a man at Flodden.

Poor Thomas was very ill when they helped him off his horse and, in spite of his mother's skill with herbs, he died of septicaemia a few days later.

To her mother's delight, Judith Heron bore a son, fathered by the Archbishop of St Andrews. The girl had no affection for the baby and it was taken over by Elizabeth, who doted on the boy and adopted him as her own. When he grew up he proved to be as wild and wicked as the Bastard, and teamed up with Elizabeth's eldest son, thieving, marauding and killing all over Northumbria.

Like all his Stewart ancestors, he did not die in his bed but in a skirmish near Otterburn, where he was killed at the age of twenty-one while laying siege to a peel tower belonging to the Percy family.

Afterword

The body thought to be that of James IV was embalmed, stitched up in leather and sent to Windsor at the cost of £14 9s 10d. Catherine of Aragon sent the tattered remains of James' surcoat to Henry VIII in France and the body was kept unburied in Sheen monastery for many years. Later it was sent to London and in the seventeenth century the head was used as a football before being buried in St Michael's churchyard.

Queen Margaret took her son James back to Stirling, where he was crowned James V on 21st September. He became the father of Mary, Queen of Scots, and died in Falkland Palace after the Battle of Solway Moss in 1542.

Margaret gave birth to another son, Alexander, in April 1514, who died in Stirling before he became an adult.

In August 1514, she precipitously married Archibald Douglas, by whom she had a daughter, but the marriage was unhappy and she began an affair with Henry Stewart. She petitioned the Pope to be allowed to divorce Douglas on the grounds that James IV had not been killed at Flodden, therefore she was not a widow when she and Douglas married.

She claimed that because no body was ever found with a chain around its waist, James survived the battle and was probably alive when she married Douglas so the marriage was invalid.

In fact many other people shared her belief that the King did not die at Flodden and there were various sightings of him. Some people claimed he had gone on pilgrimage to the Holy Land after being taken off the battlefield by three 'gentil' knights. This sounds Arthurian.

A more sinister theory spread after a skeleton bound in chains was found in the dungeon of Hume Castle, which belonged to Lord Home. It was said that Hume had taken the King captive and held him at Home till he died.

Margaret was granted her divorce and went on to marry her lover Lord Methven. In 1541 she died of a stroke at Methven Castle, Perthshire.

Lord Home was generally hated in Scotland after the terrible defeat. Three years after the battle, he and his brother were accused of treason by the remaining Scottish nobles, taken captive and executed.

The old Earl of Douglas survived the battle but went on pilgrimage to Whithorn immediately afterwards and died there of a broken heart, mourning the loss of all but one of his sons.

Abbess Isabella Hoppringle of Coldstream lost her husband, four sons and her brother, first Laird of Torwoodlee at Flodden. She continued as abbess till 1537 and was succeeded by her niece Elizabeth Hoppringle, the last abbess. In 1542 the abbey was burned down by a pack of marauding Englishmen who stole two thousand merks' worth of corn and sixty horses, and captured sixty men, which gives a clue to the richness and prosperity of the abbey.

The farm which I call Sorley's Field is near Earlston and its name is still Sorrowlessfield because all its men came back from a battle that was fought almost five hundred years ago, so strong is the memory of that tragedy.

Other farms were not so lucky. Thousands of Border men died in the battle and the only way families knew their husbands, fathers or sons were dead was because they never returned home. Their deaths went unrecorded.

The death toll among the aristocracy and

the landed gentry was recorded and was equally horrific. Nine earls out of twelve, from all parts of the country, died along with a large number of their sons and other relations. Fourteen lords of Parliament fell, as well as many abbots and superior clerics, including James' son the Archbishop of St Andrews. Edinburgh's Provost, Alexander Lauder of Blyth, and his brother died along with many burgesses from Scotland's cities.

Flodden was a disaster for the Scottish nation because it removed, not only the King, but also most of the men of power who could have influenced the course of history. Who can say if there would have been an Act of Union in 1707 if Scotland had won the battle, or even if it had never happened? On a scale of tragic after-effects, Flodden was the most devastating defeat the Scottish nation ever suffered, far worse than Culloden in 1746, because by that time Scotland was already subdued and had been sold out. In 1513, however, the country was powerful, rich and on the crest of a wave but everything crashed to disaster in only two hours.